THE CARPENTER'S SON

Book Two

Brenton G. Yorgason & Richard G. Myers

Jacket art by Aaron Fairbanks Yorgason

First printing September 1999

Library in Congress Cataloging-in-Publication Data

Yorgason, Brenton G., 1945–
The Carpenter's Son — Book Two

I. Myers, Richard G. II. Title.

ISBN 0-9659559-2-3

---

10 9 8 7 6 5 4 3 2 1

DEDICATION

To Beatrice Copley Yorgason, Brenton's mother, whose early influence and spiritual nurturing gave him a youth of hope and faith and happiness.

And, to Agnes "Kit" Walker Myers, Rick's mother, who instilled within Rick's heart a testimony of the Savior that has flourished throughout his life.

We affectionately praise the heavens for these women who gave us life. Because of their nurturing love, we learned early on to believe and trust in the Savior, Jesus Christ—even the carpenter's son from Nazareth.

ACKNOWLEDGMENTS

We thank Jason G. Yorgason, a former graduate student in the Rothberg School for Overseas Students at The Hebrew University of Jerusalem. Once again he provided significant perceptions of the Holy Land at the time of Christ's earthly ministry, as well as modern Jewish customs and beliefs. Additionally, we express appreciation for Bill and Judy Bowers, Anna Ott, Shannon Tracy, Wes and Ruth Burr, Jay and Joan Mitton, and Gladys Margetts, each of whom offered timely suggestions. Finally, we thank our ever loyal wives, Margaret and Susie, for believing as did Mary—

Authors' Note

This book, the second in what we intend will become a trilogy, begins where our book, *The Carpenter's Son,* left off. This sacred backdrop finds our fictitious friend, Jason Ellis, translating the second set of ancient scrolls entrusted in his care by the world famous Jewish rabbi, Eli Cohen. If, by chance, you have not read the aforementioned book, we strongly encourage you to do so, for it truly sets the stage for what you are now about to read.

In our first book, we took the liberty of inserting New Testament characters into the Savior's youth-filled life during events of our own imaginings that surrounded Jesus' first visit to the annual Jewish Feast of the Passover. This book, however, takes on a greater historical narrative. Extracting more from actual recorded events in the Lord's earthly ministry, we have taken a magnifying glass to these incidents, then written with our pens the enlarged perspective that each of these events provides.

As with our first book, *The Carpenter's Son*, we have not attempted to rewrite the life and history of Jesus Christ. Nor is Book Two an attempt to have thoughts and words spoken by the Savior as authoritative and accurate, although several of his quotes are as stated in the King James version of the New Testament. With this volume, our goal has again been to simply provide color and detail into the Savior's ministry, so that we might more seriously ponder and appreciate that Jesus of Nazareth, who, after all, is acknowledged as our Lord and Savior.

Part One

The Disclosure

Tel Aviv, Israel, Peace Rally

November 4, 1995

I

I am not sure why Melissa, Sid, and I decided to attend the peace rally in Tel Aviv on that fateful day when the radical student, Yigal Amir, fired the deadly shot from his handgun. But when I watched Israeli Prime Minister Yitzhak Rabin double over from the impact of the bullet, gasping in painful retreat while his life slowly waned, I was both sickened and mortified. I had grown to deeply appreciate this native-born leader. His peaceful solutions to the vast number of crises in the Middle East not only seemed viable, but appeared to have the necessary ingredients for the proposed peace accord. *Someone* needed to unify the Arab nations with their Israeli neighbors, and Mr. Rabin had been consumed with that objective.

But now, according to the police who disbursed those at the rally, he was dead.

Pandemonium erupted immediately. The scene was all too familiar, as the broad population of Jewish citizens considered Rabin a hero. After all, it was this formidable former Chief of Staff who, in 1967, led the Israelis to their dazzling six-day victory over the Egyptian-held Gaza strip and the Sinai

Peninsula. It was Rabin who wrestled the East and West Banks away from Jordan, and the Golan Heights from Syria. As far as the people were concerned, his sudden assassination was a serious blow to everything they had embodied and aspired to through the years. He had rallied primarily for freedom. During his long campaign, he had fought desperately to preserve the legacy—a veritable 'Moses' of his time.

Like the vast majority, I considered Rabin's assassination a tragic setback for the people living in this part of the world. I wondered what would become of the state of Israel and its inhabitants. At this moment of chaos, my instinct told me to leave the scene as quickly as possible, and to get my two friends and fellow students, Sid Pershing and Melissa Jones, safely back to Jerusalem.

Motioning frantically to them, I yelled, "Let's get out of here!"

Without waiting for a reply, I jumped into the driver's seat of our borrowed university car. Sensing the danger we were in, they piled into the front seat beside me, and away we went.

We drove away in complete silence, windows up, slowly making our way through thousands of grief-filled mourners as they pushed through the streets. There really wasn't much to say to one another. We were in a state of shock. We deeply respected Rabin, and thought of him as a dedicated peacemaker. Only the heavens knew how much the peace accord was needed!

As for my fellow doctoral colleagues, Sid and Melissa, I figured that they were feeling pretty much the same way I was. Sad. Desperate. Suddenly homesick.

There was a definite pit in my stomach—a gut wrenching feeling brought on by a disheveled, chaotic barrage of violence. To put it mildly, I was *terrified*!

During the next few moments of frantic, yet snail-pace

driving through the maddening crowd, I strangely detached myself from what had just transpired. Though gripped with fear, I began to reflect upon my work on the Magdalene scrolls—those dazzling papyri parchments entrusted to me by my rabbi friend and professor, Eli Cohen, of Jerusalem's Hebrew University. I couldn't help but recall the vicious and horrific events that had transpired during the life of the Savior. Not to lessen the horror of what had just happened, but through Mary Magdalene's writings in the first set of scrolls, I had been able to see into Jesus' life with a completely unique perspective . . . through the eyes of a woman! And, I might add, an extremely *articulate* scribe in her own right.

My thoughts then turned from the transcribed story of Christ's youth to the third set of scrolls. Though I had just briefly glanced at them, they contained the final days of his life and the agony of his crucifixion. During the final pain-filled hours of Christ's life while he hung there on the twisted, cruel cross, I imagined that he too felt the pains of homesickness. Like myself, he must have experienced a longing for family and loved ones that was difficult to endure. And *terrified?* My mind couldn't even fathom the depth of fear that must have engulfed him. I mean, to have my hands and feet nailed to a wooden cross, then hoisted to that hideous upright position for everyone present to see? It must have been a horror that rattled even *his* Godlike frame!

Moving away from the scene of the assassination, I wondered why God's children—so many of them through the ages—had become followers of Satan and his minions. This very day, there was at least one young fellow so vehemently opposed to the peace process in Israel that he committed murder in order to stop it in its tracks! I couldn't help but wonder what would cause *any* man to step up and commit murder? Especially a man studying law . . . one of Rabin's own society members. A Jew—

My thoughts continued, acknowledging that it had always been that way. Powerful people killing the weak, the defenseless. And the weak and defenseless, *desperate* people killing the strong and elite! Retaliation, hatred! It made me ill just to think about it. What caused the hearts of the Roman and Jewish priests of old to nail a wondrously inspired man of God to a cross made of wood, then to laugh at him while he suffered and died? Was it fear? Was it envy? Was somebody just plain and simply sadistic?

These deliberations, together with the worry for my two friends, caused me to gaze heavenward though the car's windshield and silently cry out to God for relief.

What, Father, do you see this day? Have you seen the holocaust of this moment? Have you seen the sadness of this people? Oh, dear God . . . what has happened?

Tears came unexpectedly to my eyes. I didn't completely understand them for I had never known the prime minister. Still, for whatever reason, I could not hold them back.

Melissa was sitting in the front seat next to me, while Sid—immersed in thoughts of his own—had climbed into the back of the old charcoal-grey Mercedes we had borrowed from the university. Momentarily, I became aware of Melissa watching me from out of the corner of her eye. She had seen me wiping away my tears, and had allowed a sweet, compassionate expression to draw across her face.

"Are you alright?" she whispered.

I shook my head affirmatively.

"Are you sure?"

"I'm okay," I sighed, feeling awkward by my overt emotional display, yet taken by Melissa's concern. Women were wonderful creatures. They had such delicate hearts. I was comforted by

Melissa's genuineness and sympathetic concern.

"I know," she continued, somehow reading my thoughts. "He was a good man; *Rabin*, I mean."

"He *was* a good man," I agreed. "Who knows what the people will do without him."

The thought of Rabin's absence sent a chill up my spine and into my heart. I contemplated the implications of so great a loss of leadership, and shuddered for the Jews and Palestinians left behind. For a brief instant, I felt a surge of anger. I was furious at the demented student who had taken Rabin's life. And though I was aware of the Lord's command to withhold judgment, I felt so outraged by his act of brutality that I actually *wished* for revenge—

Looking into the car's rearview mirror, I was startled to see a familiar vehicle inching closer through the turbulent frenzy of the crowded streets. It was a classic automobile, one that I recognized immediately . . . an old but immaculate cream-colored BMW 2002. To my surprise, Rabbi Eli Cohen, our professor at the university in Jerusalem, sat behind the wheel. Together with his wife Sarah and their two children, Rebecca and Joseph, they picked up speed and passed us as if we were standing still. It appeared that they too had been in attendance at the rally, and had perceived the same measure of potential post-assassination danger that had worried me.

The Cohens were such good people. The old professor had reminded me of my father, a kind and gracious man whose consistent acts of kindness made him a man without guile. Like my father, Professor Cohen was a revered and loved human being with literally hundreds of life-long friends and colleagues.

Melissa saw the Cohens, too, and tried to get their attention. But they did not see us.

I knew that Rabbi Cohen was an ardent supporter of the

prime minister, yet it was plain to see that his family's safety was paramount as he sped quickly away from the crowds and carnage. As I perceived Professor Cohen's emotional charge, I was even more uneasy than before. Slamming my foot down on the Mercedes' accelerator, I gave chase. We would follow the Cohens through the streets, stay close on their tail, and wind our way through the streets and alleyways until we were safely on the highway back to Jerusalem.

As both cars rounded a corner seconds later, a sudden volley of gunfire sounded from over our heads. It was the unmistakable rattle of an Uzi spraying its deadly slugs in heaven-only-knew which direction. Then, with what sounded like the middle of a July 4th celebration, a series of other gunshots discharged all around us—

Melissa screamed, and Sid spun around to look out the back window.

"Sidney!" Melissa yelled, "Get your *head* down!"

But Melissa's warning came too late. As Sid turned to crouch down in the back seat, a clap of gunfire slammed through the back window of the car. Sid missed being hit by the assailant's bullet by less than a fraction of an inch. Even so, a piece of shattered glass lodged itself in the left side of his head, sending him flailing backward.

A small pool of blood oozed from the wound just below Sid's left ear. It puddled, then broke free, and instantly began winding its way down the side of his cheek and neck.

"Sid!"

Melissa and I screamed his name in unison. We were certain that he had been shot.

What we *hadn't* seen was even more extreme. In the professor's car, and unbeknownst to us, two slugs had found their unlikely target. The Cohen's oldest son, Joseph, perceiving the danger of the moment, had thrown himself on top of his little sister, Rebecca.

At that very instant, I saw the gunman! He was firing from a third-story window to our right, and in an almost mysterious nanosecond of suspended time, I thought that I could actually see the bullet torpedo forth from the barrel of the gun. It shattered the rear window of the Cohen's BMW, and hit the young Cohen boy squarely in the back of the head—

"Oh, dear Lord, " I cried. "No! *Please, no!"*

The impact was immediate, for as Melissa and I watched in horror from our position alongside the Cohen's vehicle, young Joseph slumped over on top of Rebecca.

"Jason!" Melissa screamed a second time, "the professor's car! Did you see that?"

"Yes!" I shouted, very sure of what I was viewing. "Joseph is hit!"

Sid , who by now had partially recovered from the shock of being hit by the shard of glass, shook his head, trying to deal with the drunken-like instability that immersed his own body.

"What happened?" he cried out.

Neither Melissa or I could focus on his comment, so we did not reply. We were relieved to know that he hadn't really taken a bullet, for Melissa had examined him, and had found the embedded glass in the side of his face. But there was no bullet wound. She felt that he would be fine, and told me so.

Quickly, we slammed to a stop and Melissa and I jumped out of our car. Together we raced over to the stalled Cohen vehicle.

Melissa shuddered uncontrollably as she saw the extent of damage that the gunman's bullet had made. She then placed a hand over her mouth and began to cry uncontrollably.

"No!" she screamed. "Please, dear God . . . not Joseph!"

Filled with an instinctual surge of adrenaline, Joseph's

mother, Sarah, lunged from their vehicle. Opening the rear door, she hoisted Joseph from the backseat. His body was a lifeless doll-like figure with blood splattered all over his clothing.

"By the grace of God," Rabbi Cohen called out into the streets, "Joseph!"

Hurrying around the car, he pulled his son into his arms, then let out a scream that caused my own blood to curdle.

"Help us!" he cried. "Someone *please* help us!"

Then, from the corner of his eye, Rabbi Cohen saw us approach his car. A wave of relief swept over his face, and by some coincidence that couldn't have been a coincidence at all, Melissa and I took over.

From the Eyes of a Woman

II

Rabbi Eli Cohen, professor of Hebraic dialects, archeology, and theology, sat motionless. He was trying desperately to hold back the fresh batch of tears that had surfaced since our arrival at the hospital in Tel Aviv. He was tired, and was feeling his age as never before. For more than an hour he had been on his feet, pacing the waiting room of the hospital's emergency room, hoping for a miracle to occur. His mind was filled with a dreadful anticipation for the well-being of his only son, Joseph; and though the doctors had repeatedly attempted to calm him, he was less than confident about the expected outcome of the surgery. He held precariously to the hope that his remarkably brave son would survive, and eventually regain consciousness.

"Rabbi?"

At first the voice did not register. The professor had heard the familiar tone of one of his doctoral students, Melissa Jones.

"Professor Cohen?" She whispered quietly.

He turned slowly in his seat, peering at her from over his shoulder. He said nothing.

Melissa had been watching the professor pacing the floor of

the waiting room like a caged animal, and wondered if there was anything she might do to help calm the old man's nerves. She was disconcerted by the sight of this great man, for his eyes were almost swollen shut with the ongoing weeping and prolonged emotional plight that had engulfed him.

"Could I get you something, Professor?" she beckoned.

His gaze seemed far away, unaware. Though Melissa was certain that he had heard her, she pressed him again.

"Professor?"

"Thank you, my dear," he acknowledged at last, "but I'm fine." It was a feeble voice that had uttered the reply, for at the moment Rabbi Cohen was *anything* but fine. He was emotionally paralyzed with concern for his son, and the injustice that had been heaped upon his family this day.

"You look . . . well . . . ."

"*Tired,* Melissa?"

"That's not exactly what I had in mind, Rabbi," she sighed. "I was just worried, sir."

"We are all worried, my dear . . . ."

"He'll be alright," she consoled. But the professor fell silent once again, and Melissa let it go at that. She understood the kindhearted nature of Rabbi Cohen, and was grateful that they had been able to get to the hospital without further mishap. His familiarity with the streets of Tel Aviv had made it possible for both of our cars to speed to the best hospital in the city, thereby giving young Joseph a better-than-normal chance for recovery—that is, *if* there was to be a recovery.

Rabbi Cohen looked over at Melissa a moment later and, with his eyes, thanked her for her thoughtfulness. He considered Melissa, Sid, and myself friends to be admired. Over the previous three years, we had offered a courteous hand to him and his family, and he would always be grateful for that.

"I am so desperately afraid, Melissa," he said, once again requiring an old, somewhat shaken hand to rise and wipe away at the moisture that had momentarily blurred his vision.

"I understand, sir," she went on, "but I thought—"

"Listen to me, Melissa," he interpolated. "I have this awful . . . how do you say?"

"Feeling?"

"Yes," he rejoined, "it *is* a feeling. But that is not the word I have sought. It is more like a . . . premonition. I have a terrible premonition about Joseph. You see—"

Melissa bit unknowingly down onto her lower lip, then let out an audible sigh. The thought of Rabbi Cohen having disconsolate feelings about his son disturbed her deeply.

Glancing over at me, she asked, "What kind of premonition, Rabbi?"

"I should not like to say."

"Wait a minute," I interrupted. "We can't think of the worst!"

Puzzled at my sudden outburst, Sarah Cohen—who, until now, had been sitting silently nearby—focused on my words. "Yes, Jason," she interjected emphatically, and in perfect English, "We cannot . . . we *must not* give up!"

"Then I suggest that we gather together," I encouraged, "and pray for Joseph." My suggestion surprised me.

The four of us exchanged glances. Each of us were able to sense the desperation of the moment, and each realized the power of a heartfelt prayer. Who but God could intervene at this grave moment?

From all outward appearances, it was growing more and more evident that Joseph would either spend the remainder of his days in a coma, or be mercifully relieved of his life-support systems and left to pass into the world beyond. In any event, the future of young Joseph Cohen seemed hopelessly in peril.

Finding a quiet place in a shadowed corner of the hospital, we knelt on the tile floor and looked into each other's eyes. As four proclaimed Christians, we would implore the Almighty, in the name of his Holy Son, for a miracle.

The rabbi spoke with the eloquence of a prophet, humbly petitioning the Almighty. He did not read a traditional Jewish prayer, but instead prayed from the heart after a fashion that was fatherly, loving, compassionate, and ever so earnest.

"Dear God," he began hesitantly, "in our Master's name, as I have studied the translated pages of the Magdalene scrolls . . . ."

His words startled me. I had heard the old rabbi offer up a myriad of prayers since having come to know him and his family, but I had never heard him pray in the name of Christ. But he did at this moment, and the urgency with which he petitioned even the Giver of Life brought emotions to the surface that I didn't know I had.

There I was, kneeling in a small hospital room somewhere in Tel Aviv, with a closet Christian Jewish rabbi, his wife and totally silent daughter, and my friend, Melissa. The professor was praying for a miracle of such proportions that I could not even comprehend it. Nor was his prayer focused solely on his son, Joseph. He also prayed for Sid, who was also in surgery, although awake and alert to what had happened to him.

"O God, hear my words," Rabbi Cohen cried heavenward, his hands pressed inwardly together in a gesture that was so typically Christian. "Jason has finished the translation of the first set of parchments, and I cannot deny what I feel in my heart! Mary Magdalene writes of thy Holy Son. She tells of his majesty and divine being! She says that if we will follow him, we will have life everlasting—

"Dear God, my family and I are ready. We are believers. The words of Mary of Magdala speak the truth. We believe her. We believe thy will be done in all matters of urgency where thy children are concerned. Please, O God of Israel, bring our son Joseph back to us. *Please!*"

The urgency in the rabbi's prayer was extreme. Never had I heard such an impassioned plea for the soul of another. I watched with open eyes as the faith-filled professor poured out his heart to God. His bearded frame repeatedly rocked back and forward, and his white-knuckled hands shook in perfect harmony with that motion. His lips quivered as he spoke, and tears fell unabashedly from his barely visible reddened eyes.

Slowly I backed off, closed my eyes, then listened intently to the final words of his supplication. I was so joy-filled for the conversion of Rabbi Cohen. He had become a Christian, and had at least partially come out of the shadows with his conviction, allowing Melissa to understand and feel the depth of his newly discovered belief.

I was overcome by his emotional outpouring, and found my own eyes film over with moisture. Mary Magdalene, an unlikely woman of the ages, had left a written journal behind. Centuries later an esteemed Jewish rabbi reads her words and is reborn! Although I had no idea how his conversion would play itself out, I did know that it would change everything for him and his family—everything!

All Things Revealed

III

I was exhausted. A day had passed since young Joseph Cohen had been shot in Tel Aviv, and Melissa and I had returned to Eidelsen dorm, in Jerusalem. Sid had been admitted for surgery and a night of observation in the same hospital where Joseph was, and was convalescing nicely.

Prior to Melissa's and my departure from the hospital, the three of us had rallied together like latter-day soldiers, filled with a measure of hope and faith in behalf of the stricken Joseph Cohen. The Cohen family had been allowed to remain at the hospital in Tel Aviv, but Joseph had shown no signs of improvement. Instead, he had lapsed into a coma that, according to the doctors, seemed certain to either kill him or leave him permanently disabled. From what the doctors had said, if the boy lived, he would never speak again. He would never understand what had happened. He would never realize that through his timely act of unselfishness and bravery, he had literally saved the life of his little sister, Rebecca.

These facts were revealed to me by the rabbi, himself, upon

Melissa's and my return to Tel Aviv the following afternoon. We were greeted by appreciative friends, but the night of waiting had visibly taken its toll.

Then suddenly— "Rabbi?"

It was the familiar voice of the physician, Dr. Shivakumar, who had not only been a support for the family, but had been in and out of the operating room, constantly bringing up-dates of Joseph's grave condition.

"Rabbi Cohen?" the doctor called out a second time. Sitting next to me, the professor cleared his throat, ran his fingers through his silvery-grey beard, then staggered to his feet to greet the doctor. "Yes?" he managed with a raspy voice. "How is he? How is my Joseph?"

"I'm afraid that I haven't—"

"Just say the words!" the Rabbi demanded.

I could see that the old professor's hands were trembling. His wife Sarah came over to his side and ever-so-gently took his hands in her own. Tears fell spontaneously down her cheeks as she seemed to understand that the life of her son was in great peril.

"The immediate prognosis," Dr. Shivakumar disclosed, "is—"

"Is *what*?"

"There is not a great deal of hope, Rabbi."

"Of course there is hope!" the professor countered emphatically. "There will always be hope! You must try harder, all of you! He must survive! He must!"

"I assure you, sir," the confident surgeon consoled, "we're doing everything possible."

Sarah burst into tears, throwing herself back into the chair. She had been strong up to this point, but when she learned that her son might lose his life from the bullet's damaging impact, she could no longer endure. She curled into a ball and wept uncontrollably.

My roommate, Sid, had just been released, and only moments before had joined us. He had spent the night in surgery, and the doctors had sewed up the wound in his cheek where the shard of glass had been embedded. With Melissa's and my help, he had slowly reconstructed the events of the previous day. In our presence, and without knowing Joseph's condition, he had praised God that he had been spared in the random shooting. But now, with the doctor's announcement, there was sudden guilt . . . a pained expression that rose from his heart and spread across his face—

"I'm so sorry," Sid broke in. "It should have been me."

"Nonsense!" the professor scolded, turning.

"But—"

"But nothing, my friend," the Rabbi persisted. "You were spared because God willed it. All of you. Think clearly, my son. What happened here—what happened to our Joseph, what happened to *you*, what happened to Rabin . . . *everything!* It was all in the hands of God. It remains in his hands."

For a moment there was a pause in our conversation until Rabbi Cohen walked over to Sid's side, took his face in his aged and wrinkled hands, then examined the work that the Jewish doctors had done. At last he spoke. "You are most fortunate."

"Thank you, sir. I know that. If only Joseph—"

Seemingly oblivious to Sid's comment about Joseph, the rabbi added, "There is chaos on our streets. You could have been killed."

"I understand that, sir."

"The three of you must be careful," the exhausted rabbi continued, his distraction from the doctor almost complete. "You must watch yourselves. Stay away from the street rallies. Stick with your studies. Remain close to the university. Otherwise, I am afraid that—"

"You will frighten them, Eli," Sarah interrupted.

"Better to be frightened than to be dead—"

The professor's comment struck deep. Melissa and I were standing away from him and Sid as they exchanged words, but it was so true—everything he said. We might very well have been killed, and the thought of that unsavory fact left me feeling vulnerable and afraid. I suddenly wished that I was safely back in the states. Homesickness was definitely having its way with me.

Leaving Sid and Melissa to comfort the Cohens, I retired to a nearby waiting room, found a sofa, and closed my eyes. The last day had been taxing beyond belief. While the doctors worked to save the life of young Joseph Cohen, I soon found myself drifting off into a uniquely blissful dream.

Like so many times these days, my dreamscapes centered around the colorful world of Mary of old . . . Mary from the ancient city of Magdala. It then switched to the present, and became almost a subconscious review of the events of the past hour. Floating in and out of an awakened state, I began to chart what had transpired.

For weeks now, other than the professor, himself, I had been the only one to work on the translation of the ancient artifacts found by Professor Eli Cohen's father. It was a document we were now calling The Magdalene Scrolls. And though the experience was more pleasure than it was work, I was nevertheless anxious to include both Sid and Melissa in translating the final two sets of scrolls. In fact, just days earlier I had convinced the good rabbi to allow that very thing to happen.

Only two days previous, before the chilling designs of the Adversary were set into motion, I was given notice that the two of them would not only be allowed to assist me with the second set of scrolls, but would be able to examine and become familiar with the first record as well.

What a relief!

And now, only minutes before, Rabbi Cohen had told Melissa and Sid about the three sets of ancient scrolls found by his father, in 1946, just weeks after the Dead Sea Scrolls were found. He also related how he had met with me at the traditional site of John Mark's home, which was rebuilt after the Roman slaughter of Christians between 67 and 71 A.D. He said that it was inside this same home that historians felt Jesus had held his Last Supper with the twelve biblical apostles.

"Do you think it happened there?" Melissa had probed, wanting to feed her appetite with information and further insights.

"Oh yes," the rabbi confirmed. "It was also in the foundation of this ancient home that my father found these scrolls—these records, if you will—that had been written by none other than one of Jesus' closest friends, Mary from Magdala."

"But—" Melissa questioned.

"It is all true, my dear," he assured her, realizing the intensity of her and Sid's astonishment. As he continued the tale, smiling genuinely, he reminded them of the importance of temporarily keeping the find and all of the elements of the tale secret.

"But why, Professor?" Sid protested. "Why not tell the whole world!"

Carefully giving thought to his every word, Rabbi Cohen slowly replied, "As you know, Jason has been . . . how do you say? Oh, yes, I believe the word is *discreet.*"

I nodded my head in affirmation.

"He has not discussed the contents of his dissertation with either of you—that is, not until Sunday last. Until then, you knew only that he was working on a project with me, and that this project was confidential. Of course, there *is* a reason for this."

"A reason?" Sid pressed, while patting the bandage on his

cheek. "What reason, Rabbi?"

A soft and comforting smile spread across the professor's wrinkled face as he continued to reveal the content of the ancient scrolls to my colleagues. He seemed relieved to be able to tell someone "new" about the secrets he had kept hidden for so many years. But he could never know how relieved *I* was that the scrolls were finally coming to the surface. For indeed, I had desperately wanted to share my translating experiences with both Melissa and Sid, but had been unable to do so. Again Sid questioned the rabbi's reason for secrecy.

"There are many reasons," Professor Cohen smiled. "Jason has just completed the translation of the first of three sets of scrolls, and it will become his dissertation. He is now preparing to present the project to the committee at the university."

"Committee?" Melissa probed further. "You mean his doctoral committee?"

"Not exclusively. Two mornings from now Jason will tell the world through a much expanded committee of orthodox professors and administrators, as well as the press—"

"Wait a minute!" I interrupted, "You said that you were going to meet with the university administrators first, Rabbi, and inform them of the scrolls."

"Yes, Jason," he assured me, "and I mean to do just that. Do not worry. Today is *Shabbat* for our people . . . our day of worship. But tomorrow is the day my family and I will privately worship our Lord, even here in the hospital. Tomorrow is the Lord's Sabbath. It is fitting that the three of us be here with our Joseph, even though he is unaware of our presence.

"I will not be able to reveal my family's conversion to Christ at the university, of course, for the professional implications of doing so would be irreparable. You could not know how much—any of you. Yet, as painful as my silence must be, it is preferred to the alternative consequences, especially for the security of my family.

"It is . . . how shall I say . . . difficult for me to acknowledge the Lord of Heaven, and not be able to reveal this wondrous knowledge to my colleagues. I am ashamed, my young friends, that silence must be my expression. There *is* no other way. I must be able to provide for my family, and to insure their safety. An acknowledgment of Jesus' Messiahship would cause us problems beyond our ability to endure."

"And Sarah?" Melissa interjected honestly. "She too has been converted to Christianity? I mean . . . is that what you're telling us? You and your family are now believers in the divinity of Christ? You, who are Jews?"

The seasoned rabbi looked deeply into Melissa's eyes, then held his head high. It was plain to see that he was not ashamed of the truth he had come to know. While he had shared the good news with me in the ancient Garden of Gethsamene, I had not passed along the information to anyone.

"Perhaps I should admit," Sarah suddenly interjected, her weathered face sobered even more, "that I gained a testimony of Jesus' identity several weeks before Eli did. I read through the translation of the scrolls Jason was working on. I call it my woman's intuition. My heart has known the truth of Mary's words from the start."

Melissa and I exchanged glances. Sid stood back away from all of us with a hand tucked up under his chin.

"Even my little ones . . . not so little anymore . . . " the professor added, calmly thinking through his stream of thought, "they too were able to grasp hold of the inspiring words of this remarkable scribe, Mary of Magdala. They know that her words are true, even as I know them to be so. In their youth, they have felt the power of the divine one! They have . . . how did you say it, Jason? They have received—"

"Testimonies?"

"Yes, that is the expression—testimonies! My children, my wife, and now myself! Each of us have been given these precious affirmations from God. And why? Why did these things happen to us . . . to a family of devout orthodox Jews? Do you think it is by accident?"

"I . . . I don't know what to think, Professor," Melissa replied shyly. "But I do know that I am thrilled for you . . . all of you. It's wonderful."

"As am I, Rabbi," I confirmed, my heart leaping with delight as the old teacher's enthusiasm bellowed forth like a symphony, seemingly detached from the life and death peril of his son, Joseph.

Standing to stretch the old muscles in his body, Professor Cohen looked at the fluorescent lights that hung above us in the hospital's ceiling, then gave an audible sigh. We were captivated by the change in our instructor's heart, and wondered how it could have been possible for such a wonder to transpire. A miracle had taken place. It wasn't every day that a renowned orthodox Jewish scholar announced his conversion to Christendom. And to do it at the most crucial hour of his family's life made it even that much more extraordinary.

With the tenderness of a loving father, the old rabbi shuffled over to where Melissa and Sid were sitting. He was shaking from what I expected was the turmoil of the recent hours of anguish and concern, but was as kind as ever as he began to speak.

"You know," he began, searching the eyes of my two friends, "it was at Jason's request that I have allowed you both to take an active part in his project . . . ."

Sid and Melissa exchanged glances then turned toward me for

some sort of affirmation. I shook my head ever so slightly, giving them what they needed.

Seeming to read their thoughts, the rabbi continued. "You will make a formidable team, especially after the two of you have completed your dissertations. But I feel there are things you should understand before you actually get started on the second set of scrolls. The information inside these parchments . . . it is not mine, but ours—Jason's and mine. And now it will be yours as well."

The rabbi's voice choked, and a tear formed in the corner of one of his eyes.

"Forgive me," he requested, again clearing his throat. "You see, Jason and I have just completed the four most sobering months of our lives—in translating the first of Mary's three records. You will both be very proud of him, for he has been challenged to oversee the work in its entirety. He is in charge of these scrolls. It was a promise I made to my father while he lay on his deathbed, and which is now being fulfilled. I was to listen to the Holy Spirit, then tutor and present these parchments to the right Christian so that he might translate them. When I selected Jason for this task, I knew that I had fulfilled my promise with integrity."

"I feel so . . . honored," Melissa echoed honestly.

"As do I," Sid followed.

The staggering implications of the experience—and now of this moment—were almost more than either could assimilate.

For a full hour, and with no further word about Joseph, the three of us listened with rapt interest as the professor rehearsed the events that had led up to the finding and eventual translation of the Magdalene scrolls. I was comforted to know that I would no longer be alone in this tediously revealing process; but that, instead, I would have the assistance of my closest American friends.

My dreamscape was beginning to fade when I heard Melissa's voice. "Jason," she shouted, while running into the room, "we must get a doctor!"

Professor Cohen had passed out. The mounting anxiety of his not knowing the eventual fate of his son, coupled with the lamentable assassination of his country's leader, had finally taken its toll on our aging mentor. While Melissa returned to help the rabbi, I jumped up and retrieved the same doctor who had been caring for the needs of his son, Joseph. The exhausted professor was revived within a matter of minutes. However, at the request of his wife, Sarah, as well as the medical staff, the three of us were asked to leave the hospital and return to Jerusalem.

We did as we were instructed, and after having a further prayer with Rabbi Cohen and his family, we quietly left them in their beleaguered vigil.

An hour later, after an uneventful ride from Tel Aviv, we wound our way through the hills toward Jerusalem. Arriving on French Hill near the university, we grabbed a quick lunch of falafels on Lehi Street. It was our favorite hangout, an Arab-owned corner food stand near the Hyatt Regency hotel. After eating, we gathered across the street in Sid's and my apartment, in Eidelsen dorms. We immediately began reading through a copy of the first set of scrolls.

Sid and Melissa—although unusually quiet—appeared delighted to have been introduced to the artifact. They were as eager as I was to begin the work. Nevertheless, assuming Professor Cohen could return to Jerusalem, there was the meeting that still needed to be attended to on the morrow. Although I wasn't altogether comfortable about the expected outcome of the rare public announcement, I agreed with the professor that the parchments should be shown to the world before we continued the translation of the next journal record.

As for Rabbi Cohen and his family, they were convinced to return to their home on Bar Kochva Street, and to wait there for further word on their comatose Joseph. They would get a good night's rest, then return to Tel Aviv following the press conference.

The following morning's unprecedented announcement proceeded, as scheduled, with Rabbi Cohen providing a requested "no progress" update on his son, Joseph. Then, without taking questions, he made his startling announcement to Hebrew University's administration and faculty. I sat quietly at a small adjoining table with the ancient artifacts at my side.

Melissa was also in attendance, although she seemed strangely distant, almost detached, and smiled weakly as she passed me and took her seat in the back of the room. I wondered about that, but concluded that the previous forty-eight hours had simply taken their toll on her. She didn't look like her normal self. Instead, her shoulder-length hair was done in a ponytail, and she looked as sullen as could be.

In spite of her condition, I was appreciative that Melissa had made the effort to attend the late morning announcement. Even so, I was concerned that Sid was nowhere to be found. He was up and dressed when I left the dorm, and while he acted uncharacteristically aloof, I had taken his behavior to be a result of his accident. He looked pale, and simply nodded as I bid him farewell, reminding him that I would save a seat for him at the scroll's announcement.

The esteemed Rabbi Cohen, meanwhile, was fully prepared to be reprimanded for not having disclosed the existence of the ancient scrolls until this time. However, the fact that he was complying with the deathbed request of his equally revered rabbi father, gave him the professional reprieve he had hoped for.

What *I* wasn't prepared for, of course, was the sudden discomfort on the faces of the orthodox Jews present. Two of them, elderly professors who were in their final year of teaching before retirement, appeared to be especially distraught. They made no comment, but appeared unsettled as their eyes glanced suspiciously at the three sets of scrolls on the table. I felt their uneasiness and sensed that the existence of the scrolls had hit a nerve. It was the nerve of knowledge that a contemporary corroboration revealed that Jesus of Nazareth was, in fact, the promised Messiah.

Their whisperings back and forth were in their native Hebrew, so I could only make out part of what they actually said. What I knew, for sure, was that they were shaken to the core.

I was ashamed that I had allowed even the slightest bit of anger to infiltrate my heart over the matter, especially since I understood the nature of their religious convictions. It was a revelation that was both un-reassuring and painful for these orthodox Jews. And to think that 2,000 years earlier their forefathers erroneously rejected his Messiahship. The consequences of this near-universal decision led to a sadness in their countenances—a perceptible void of the Savior's light—and then perpetuated itself in the persecution they had experienced since then. What a tragedy!

Other than this almost unnoticed side dialogue, for me the surprise moment in the meeting was when the university president introduced me to the group. He did this while dramatically waving my dissertation proposal in the air. He then called on me to present my proposal for approval. I was to share my translating experience of the previous semester.

I knew that I was among a unique gathering of Jewish

scholars, and because of what I had been witnessing among the two skeptical professors, I chose not to focus on the Christian theme of the scrolls. Instead, I arose and presented them as well-preserved historical documents. I declared them to be parchments that were written by the hand and heart of a woman—then let it go at that. I also spoke of the singular experience of working at the side of the esteemed Rabbi Cohen. I then paid tribute to his lifelong integrity with the find, as well as to his competency as a scholar of ancient Hebraic writings.

While my exuberance was clearly evident—even though the Jewish scholars seemed almost detached from Rabbi Cohen's disclosure of Christian artifacts—I felt a new level of confidence with each word that rolled off my tongue. Although outright rejecting any credence to who Christ was, it was clear that my new colleagues were accepting of me, and of the task I was performing. The university president, who was also the voice at the microphone with me, dealt with this issue deftly. Rejecting any claim that the ancient author made about Christ, he flatly stated that her impressions were hers, alone—those of a flawed woman. That part bothered me a lot.

Even with these comments, as I concluded my remarks a warm wave of relief passed over me. A vote was taken, and I was unanimously declared "Doctoral *Candidate* Ellis," rather than "Jason Ellis, the doctoral student." This final pre-doctorate acknowledgment made all the effort of the previous three years worthwhile. My course work was finished, and now my dissertation proposal had been accepted by the powers that be.

Feeling free of worry regarding the Christian content of the scrolls, my next step would be to write a summary of the first set of writings, and do so in dissertation format. I would then defend the same, and if successful, would receive my Ph.D., or doctor of philosophy degree. It was a dream that was becoming more a reality with every passing month.

As the meeting wound to a close, a second vote was taken. It was determined that I would likewise be given permission—with Melissa and Sid assisting—to continue translating the final two sets of scrolls. Concern was expressed that such involvement would hamper the conclusion of my colleagues' dissertations, but Professor Cohen convinced his colleagues that he would monitor and limit both Sid and Melissa's involvement until their own dissertations and oral exams were completed. Each had successfully completed their comprehensive written exams, and they were well into the meat of their dissertations. In fact, both of them had become doctoral candidates the previous semester, well ahead of me.

A sense of uneasiness was also present regarding the safety of the scrolls, even though they smacked of a false Christ. It was determined that, after photographing and microfilming the ancient records, they would be kept in their original containers, in the university library vault. Besides Rabbi Cohen and the recorders, only Melissa, Sid, and I were to be allowed access to them.

Following this procedure, they reasoned, the continuity of the find would remain intact. In addition, premature and possibly inaccurate disclosures would not take place. Such exclusive access would insure a pure and scholarly approach to the translation, and would maintain the fidelity they felt was owed to the ancient record keeper—even if she were a woman, a follower of "the great pretender," as some of them called him, Jesus of Nazareth.

How often I had to bite my tongue . . . for these scholars seemed so callous and indifferent to anything out of the norm, even pompous and arrogant like the scribes and Pharisees of old.

As the meeting adjourned, everyone gathered around my table. Rabbi Cohen directed them to examine the three sets of scrolls, as well as the ancient container. After considerable thought, he had still determined not to reveal the existence of the Lazarus staff. Instead, because he had previously given it to me, it would remain my personal, undisclosed gift. After all, his father had instructed him to listen to the Holy Spirit, and to dispose of the ancient artifacts as he deemed appropriate.

The rabbi later told me that I had earned the permanent right to this gift relic, and that it would likely be taken from me if its existence were made known. I thought much about this staff from then on . . . always wondering what to do with it. It wasn't something that I felt should be dragged around in any public place or even exposed to the elements of the outdoors. This was a sensational object of historical value . . . worth a thousand times its weight in gold. Often the thought occurred to me that it should be placed in a sacred hiding place, perhaps at one of the museums. At the moment, however, I did not know where to put it.

I did, however, show the impressive crafted piece to both Sid and Melissa upon our return from Tel Aviv. They were simply astounded.

After the meeting at the university, Melissa and I planned on returning immediately to the hospital, in Tel Aviv, to visit young Joseph. Sid had expressed that he was not feeling well from his own accident, and so had remained bedfast in our dorm.

To Melissa's and my surprise, instead of going back to Tel Aviv with the professor's family, we were escorted to the Cohen home for a hastily prepared noon-day meal. Seating ourselves in the formal front room, Sarah Cohen entered, wiping her hands on her well-worn apron.

"Joseph would want us to celebrate this moment with you," she declared, her eyes revealing the graveness of the hour, and the sleepless ordeal her family was still in the midst of.

In spite of her haggard condition, Sarah appeared elegant—very regal, dark-haired, and ever so kind and hospitable. Even with what she had been through, she had an olive complexion that radiated warmth and love in an almost iridescent manner.

As Sarah spoke, I was reminded of my appreciation for Rabbi Cohen's resolve to have his family always speak in English—clearly their second language—whenever in our presence. Although Melissa and I had both become quite proficient in speaking modern Hebrew, it was a gesture we appreciated. Besides, it gave them a forum in which to practice their English.

After a troubled night of sleep, Sarah had spent the entire morning preparing the meal. In spite of the Cohen family crisis, the two of us were honored to be there. Regardless of her brother's condition, Rebecca seemed happy, showering us with gifts she had made. These were drawings that depicted images of Jesus' life as she had only recently begun to understand him.

The obvious cloud on the luncheon was the gnawing pain that each of us felt for young Joseph who continued to linger in a paralyzed state of unconsciousness. Sarah, in particular, seemed the most preoccupied with the precarious nature of her son's life. It was plain to see that her heart was filled with anguish. For some reason, little Rebecca assumed her father's peace-filled state of reliance upon God's will.

"Sarah," I whispered, "are you okay?"

She replied that she had faith, and had total reliance in Christ's will regarding her Joseph; but she also said that she didn't feel well. Sensing her turmoil, I could not help wondering how she could be so hospitable.

And so the noon-day meal was eaten, an hour and a setting that I will remember for as long as I live. When it was time for us to go, Rabbi Cohen made a pronouncement.

"My dear friends, I thank you for your prayers, and for your thoughtfulness to my family, especially to my Joseph. He is in the Lord's hands now, and we must continue in the faith Sarah spoke of. She and Rebecca will be driven back to Tel Aviv, and there they will remain to encourage our Joseph in his slumber. For the rest of us, it is my thought that we petition God for his mercy; and then that we begin what we have been asked to do—the translating of Mary's second parchment. It is my request. I would like to meet you at the library at precisely 2:00 P.M."

Sensing that we were to obey, even though we had planned on returning to Tel Aviv, we agreed to the meeting. Without lingering, we thanked Sarah and Rebecca for dinner, and excused ourselves.

Little could I have anticipated the bombshell that awaited me in the next hour—

Walking slowly along Mevo Harari Street, we took the shortcut route back to the dorms. I didn't feel like talking. Instead, I silently reflected on the experience we had just shared. I also thought of my deceased wife, Kirsten, and the strength of loneliness I had felt for her since Rabin's death. Suddenly I was aware of Melissa's unusual silence. She hadn't spoken a word since leaving the Cohen's home, and that wasn't like her. She was obviously disturbed about Joseph. Although I was concerned about his fate, I had felt the power of the Cohen family's faith. Somehow, against all odds, I knew a miracle would take place in his behalf.

At that moment a small herd of Bedouin-owned sheep passed by, stirring the caked ground at the side of the street into loose dirt granules. Melissa motioned for us to sit down on a rock fence, facing the path that led to the university. She, for some reason, continued her uncharacteristically somber behavior. Even with Joseph Cohen's precarious condition, it just wasn't like her. There was an emotion present that I had sensed earlier, and although I didn't know what was on her mind, I found myself wanting to reach out to her and offer moral support.

"Hey," I whispered quietly, "are you alright, Missy?"

She lifted her head slightly, absently gazing at me with her emerald-green eyes. She then replied matter-of-factly, "Sure, Jase. I'm fine."

Reaching out to lift her up, I suggested that we get moving again toward the university.

"You know, Melissa," I coughed, "I've been particularly homesick the past few weeks. Still, I wouldn't trade the past several months for anything in the world. Sitting at Rabbi Cohen's side while translating the Mary parchments has given me the most profound appreciation for not only the historical aspects of the work, but for Jesus Christ, personally. I feel like I've been inside an unreal world of sorts—a world of the ancients. I've had the opportunity of seeing through their eyes; a time that, for way too many, has been long forgotten."

Without looking at me, Melissa drew in a deep breath of fresh air. She was so beautiful, and our friendship was nothing less than a godsend. As I watched her auburn-colored hair dancing gently in the wind, I was—in spite of my deepest fears—becoming intoxicated by her presence. These stirrings, coming more often these days, and with greater intensity, produced a measure of guilt that I could not deal with. My childhood sweetheart and bride, Kirsten, had unexpectedly passed away from an aneurysm over three years earlier. Even though I had finally resolved Kirsten's absence, still I felt the void of her death, and longed to hold her in my arms and feel the love that we shared. I didn't tell Melissa, of course, but it was Kirsten I had missed the most these past few months.

I needed her. I missed her. Yet as I beheld Melissa's presence, I wandered in and out of a fantasy that saw us together; holding each other, as Kirsten and I had done, and even sharing our lives.

These newly planted competing emotions, together with a deep and powerful sense of loyalty that still existed for my beloved departed, gave birth to an increased level of guilt that was crippling. If I allowed my feelings for Melissa to grow, I would perhaps be setting myself up for another serious emotional blow if something were to happen to *her*.

But, why? Why was I feeling this way? I knew, as my parents back in Austin, Texas, had counseled, that I could not—and would not—remain single for the rest of my life. I had far too much to share with someone. Life was difficult enough all by itself, and for that reason, I always hoped that I would eventually meet someone new. Part of me hoped that another woman would come into my life. I wanted it to be so, for life was not meant to be spent in the shadows of loneliness.

"Jason?"

"Huh . . . what?" I stammered. The clamor of Melissa's voice brought me back to the here and now.

"You were speaking of your dissertation, Jase; your appreciation for the ancient records."

"Ah, yes," I went on, refocusing my thoughts. "It is as though I have begun to examine Christ's life in technicolor for the very first time!"

"I'll bet."

"Really, Melissa," I insisted, "I can't believe the emotions I've been dealing with. The whole story, the parchments, the find. It's extraordinary!"

"Not to mention the professor's trust in you," Melissa added proudly. "It's all pretty amazing, Jason."

"That's what I'm talking about."

Pressing further, her questions came in rapid fire. "So, what about me? Where do I fit in? Are we really going to work as a team the way Rabbi Cohen has spoken of? After all, my dissertation is nearly written."

Melissa's words filtered out into the stillness of the early afternoon. It was odd that no one had passed us on the road since we had stopped to rest.

Glancing toward her, I perceived an unexpected furrow in her brow. As I considered her unusually pensive expression, she suddenly turned away.

"What's wrong?" I asked. She didn't reply.

"Melissa?" Still, nothing.

I was troubled that I might have said something to disturb her, but I couldn't figure out what that might have been. So once more I turned my complete attention to this uniquely special colleague and friend, and pressed her further. "Missy, is something bothering you . . . I mean, other than Joseph Cohen's condition?"

"Jason," she snapped, "there's something I must tell you."

Startled with the tone of her voice, I recovered to ask, "Yes?"

"I have something to tell you that I'm sure you'll find hard to believe."

"Okay," I said, suddenly feeling her concern. "I'm game. What is it?"

"It's about Sid . . ." she replied slowly.

"Yes? What about him?"

All at once, Melissa burst into tears and buried her face in her lap. It was obvious that she was distraught, but other than the remarkably unlikely acts of violence in Tel Aviv, for the life of me I couldn't understand why.

"Sid's gone back to the states, Jason. He left this morning."

"Say *what?*"

"It's why I was almost late for your announcement. He left a letter on my dorm door, and I had to read it. *I'm* the reason he left."

"Excuse me?" Melissa had a pained expression, and she found it difficult to look at me. "What are you talking about, Missy?" I probed. "What do you mean, *you're* the reason he left?"

"Well," she sighed hesitantly, and with obvious discomfort, "I . . . I've not told you this, Jason, but last night Sid asked me to marry him."

"*He what!*"

Startled by my spontaneous response, she looked safely back at her feet, and continued. "I know it sounds crazy, but last night after we returned from Tel Aviv, Sid came over and . . . well, he proposed to me."

"Wait a minute, Missy! You're kidding, right?"

"I wish I were."

I was completely taken back by her announcement, and had no response to this startling bombshell. Marriage? Sid and Melissa? I couldn't believe it—

"He said that he'd had feelings about me for some time," she continued, pretending not to notice my surprise, "but just hadn't been able to tell me."

"You and Sid?" I again questioned sarcastically. "Come on! You guys haven't even dated . . . or . . . wait a minute! Have you?"

"No more than you and I have," she sighed. "Well, maybe a little. We have spent a lot of time together, talking."

"I can't believe what I'm hearing."

"I'm trying to tell you, Jase, Sid wanted to marry me; it's just that simple. It's hard enough to spit it out, especially while looking at that cute little Kevin Costner look of yours."

What was Melissa saying? What hidden messages? Her statement sent more signals than I could assimilate, for the three of us had been almost inseparable for the previous three years. Still, neither Sid *or* I had even hinted at dating Melissa, let alone acted upon it. It was an almost unwritten creed that we would just be friends. And that Costner stuff again? Why on earth had she brought up my often-joked-about appearance? It had been months since she and Sid had teased me about looking like the actor, Kevin Costner. They said that I had his boy-like grin, and all; but what did that have to do with *now?* Or with *her? Was she hiding something from me?* For no apparent reason, I found myself dangling on the edge of sheer panic.

But why?

As Melissa's words reverberated again and again through my mind, I found it useless to even try to respond. When I finally did, my query seemed hollow and strangely intruding—

"So . . . what did you tell him, Melissa?"

Forcing her eyes to look into mine, she was barely able to whisper. "I . . .uh . . . told him that I could never marry him. In fact, I told him that I didn't know if I was capable of marrying *anyone*, not just him."

"Oh?"

"He didn't pursue it," she continued with an innocent girlish tone in her voice. "But he did say that he understood, and that he wouldn't press the issue further if I was truly that resolute in my feelings."

"Really?"

"That was how it ended. I haven't spoken to him since. I will say that, given the circumstances, he felt that leaving now would remove any discomfort of you and I working together on the scrolls. He also said that he could complete his dissertation from his home in the states, then fly back for his oral exams."

"He just packed up after I left our room?"

"Yes, he said it was best that way. He couldn't think of how to tell you good-bye. He said it was too painful, and that you would understand. He is going to write. He was taking a taxi to Tel Aviv, and was going to see Joseph before heading to the airport. He was as resolute as I've ever known him to be."

As I tried to grasp what Melissa had just said, she sat straight up, and stretched her back and shoulders. Quite suddenly, with a new gush of tears working down around her cheeks, she blurted, "You can't understand, Jason!"

"What? Now what—?"

"You'll never understand! Ever! You and your wife had everything, you did everything right—even if you were only together for a short while. On the other hand, I betrayed all the trust that God gave me."

"Did things right? Betrayed God? What are you talking about? Melissa, you're one of the most remarkable— "

"*Stop it!*" she demanded, spinning around to face me.

For a moment, I was stunned. I couldn't understand a word she was saying. But then, recognizing the pain and the fear that suddenly flashed in her eyes, I did just that. I shut up long enough to give some serious thought to the whole situation before me. I had never been so at a loss for words, and I had no idea how to help her through whatever it was she was dealing with. At least, not until—

"You see, Jason," she pleaded, her hands shaking as she held them over her mouth, "I gave birth. I had a . . . a . . . baby girl the year before I came to Jerusalem. As if that weren't enough, out of fear I gave my sweet little baby daughter up for adoption!"

"You *what?"*

"I gave her away, Jason. I forever gave my daughter away."

Melissa's anguish was suddenly more strenuous than even she

could bear. She again burst into a flowing fountain of tears. Her eyes had a petrified look, and for just a moment seemed to teeter on the edge of a breakdown.

"Oh, Jason . . ." she cried out, her words muffled and incoherent. She looked longingly up into my eyes, then said seven words that would forever haunt— "I never even got to *hold* her!"

It was clear that I was wading through deep waters with Melissa. Her facial expressions changed drastically. One moment she had been her typical good-natured self, with all of the enthusiasm of a best friend. Then suddenly she was a basket case. She was filled with a turmoil that I could not understand. There was a high-crested panic in her voice that frightened me to the core. I thought that I would do well to whisk her off to a doctor somewhere—a psychologist, a psychiatrist, anyone in the counseling profession. Still, I had no idea where to go.

Taking Melissa's shoulders in my hands, I drew her close. She resisted only briefly, then threw her arms around me and sobbed uncontrollably. After several moments of muffled silence, she pulled back and looked searchingly up into my eyes. Her makeup—what was left of it—had smeared itself down across her cheeks, giving her an almost sinister appearance.

"You know, Jason," she tried to speak with a measure of control in her unsteady voice, "I didn't even know who the father was! He could have been . . . well, there were two—"

"Shhhhh," I whispered, placing my fingers over her lips. "It's okay, Missy. You'll be alright, I promise."

"History repeated itself, Jason; for I've never known who *my* father was!"

I drew her to me again, this time allowing my fingers to pass through her hair while I cradled her head as I would an innocent child starving for affection. Her revelations, spoken from the depths of years of a harrowed-up heart, tore at the core of my soul. My emotions were sympathetic, yet were in no way judgmental. A feeling within me began to rise to the surface—a feeling of unconditional love. I was suddenly very aware of her needs, and cared for her in a completely compassionate way. Furthermore, more than anything else in the world I wanted to tell her that I loved her. I wanted to tell her that I was in love *with* her.

Was I going nuts? How could I betray Kirsten like this? How could I possibly be falling in love with someone new . . . someone so unstable?

Then suddenly—at the very moment I felt as if I could do nothing more than cry with her—an unexpected peace swept over my heart. My mind moved away from my own feelings, and I was given to understand the true power of the Savior's atonement. I saw myself as a much needed comforter. I was caught up in the thought of Jesus' divine love for me, for Melissa, for all of God's children, and I wondered what he would say to her in this moment of need. He too would provide comfort. He too would put his arms around her and tell her that all was well . . . that all would be alright.

"I . . . I'm so ashamed, Jason," she rambled on, tormenting herself with every word. "I feel utterly and completely unworthy. I am not deserving in the least. To be here, I mean, learning of the greatest man that ever lived. *Jesus!* If anything, I think my presence here will hinder the work—your's and the professor's translating. I'll put a vexing spell on it; I just know I will."

"Cut it out, Melissa," I interrupted, but she wouldn't stop criticizing herself.

"Honestly, Jase . . . I don't even feel like I should be called your friend. You and Kirsten did everything right, and all I've been able to do is mess things up. The Savior wouldn't have anything to do with me now. I might as well have pounded the nails into his wrists."

"Stop it, Melissa!" I demanded, again trying to defuse the cacophony of escalating madness. But still, the words fell upon deaf ears.

"For years," she insisted, pretending not to hear, "I've been trying to feel his forgiveness, like everything would be alright. Instead, I look into the mirror every morning . . . every night. I only think of how much I hate myself! I can't stand the image that stares back at me!"

"Now, hold on—" I insisted, thinking how I might lay to rest her emotions. Yet for the moment, the only question I could think to ask was whether she had given her past to Christ.

"Have you given yourself to the Lord? Have you prayed for his grace?"

What made me think of saying that? I hadn't ever used those expressions before. But somehow I knew that she desperately needed to get down on her knees and pray.

"Pray?" she replied sternly. "I can't even kneel down, Jason, let alone *pray!*"

Searching, pleading to know how to console her, I closed my eyes and waited for an answer.

Time stood still. The moment was maddening. I felt helpless and lost. Though I wanted desperately to do something, or say something that would provide for her even the smallest degree of hope, I couldn't utter a single word—

Nothing would come into my mind!

Desperately I ached for that still, small voice that I'd been taught about all of my life—a quiet whispering that was supposed to enter into my soul—a celestial directional to provide me with the words to say.

Please, Father, I petitioned silently, *is there something thou would have me say? Is there—*

Then suddenly I knew!

My eyes deceived me for the moment, for as they filled with the moisture of gratitude that came streaming into my heart, I saw blurred images of one of the two most beautiful women I'd ever known. Melissa, standing timidly before me, looked like an angel sent down from the very clouds of heaven. She was simply radiant—

"Listen to me, Melissa," I declared, my heart brimming with renewed hope, "*I* will pray! I'll pray, and ask the Lord for you. I mean . . . well . . . if it's alright with you, I can pray in your behalf."

"Oh, no, Jason," she resisted, "that would just make me feel worse!"

"But, why?"

"I don't know," she responded feebly. "Maybe it's because one person *can't* pray for another's sins . . . or pay for them."

"Now that's a silly thing to say," I countered. "I mean, think about it, Missy. What do you think the Savior's mission was all about?"

As Melissa looked at me in recognition of what I had just said, she exclaimed, "But I can't go to him, Jason! I'm too ashamed!"

"Then I'll pray and ask him to send his Holy Spirit to give *you* the strength to go to him."

"You'd do that for *me*?"

"In a second. We're best friends, aren't we?"

"Of course."

"Then, it's settled. I'll call on the Father for you. That is, I'll make that request on one condition."

"Condition?"

"Yes, I'll do it," I smiled warmly, while wiping my own tears, "on the condition that you will pray for *me*."

"What?"

"That's right, Missy. You acknowledged that we were best friends. And since we both agree on that, well, maybe you could pray for me, too."

Questioning honestly, she asked, "But, what on earth for?"

"Well," I replied sincerely, "you could ask God to forgive me of my sins as well."

"*Your* sins?" she countered, looking a bit startled, "What are you talking about, Jason Ellis? What sins do you have to repent of?"

"My dear Missy," I breathed tenderly, "do you think that you are the only one in this world with such heavy weights to bear? I need some of that heavenly strength just as you do. I want you to pray that I'll have the ability to repent of *my* sins. I have them, you know . . . just as everyone does. You're not alone, Melissa Jones—not by any means!"

Melissa again looked up into my eyes, this time searching every square inch of them. Tears fell unashamed down across her cheeks.

"Oh, Jason," she said with the warmth of a cozy candle on a moon lit night. "Hold me, please. Don't say anything more; just hold me."

And so I did, again brushing her hair with my fingers as my mind seemed to float absently in the ever-so-splendid silence of the moment. It was a feeling I would always cherish, and one that, for the life of me, I did not want to end.

Moments later, however, Melissa pulled away from me and at last smiled. She stood gracefully, then reached down to her knees and brushed away the dirt from her Levi jeans.

"You are the kindest man I have ever known, Jason. Your thoughtfulness has given me a new strength. With all my heart, I thank you."

"You're so welcome, Missy." And although I wanted to stand and hold her more than I already had, she again wiped her face, then reminded me of the professor.

"Rabbi Cohen— Won't he be expecting us? I almost forgot. We're supposed to meet him back in the university archives."

Silent and pensive moments later, Melissa and I arrived at the guard post at Hebrew "U". All around us olive trees of archaic origin rustled in the breeze, creating an almost magical feel to the afternoon. Then, quite unexpectedly, a lizard sprinted across the path in front of us and Melissa jumped backwards.

"Whoa!" she shouted, grabbing hold of me. "What was that?"

"Just a little ol' reptile," I reassured her. "Nothing you should worry about."

She raised a hand to her face and wiped away the tears that had fallen earlier. "How do my eyes look?" she inquired, wondering if all the crying she'd done during our conversation had made a mess of her make up.

"You're as beautiful as ever, Missy. Besides, I don't think Professor Cohen will be concerned about—"

"Concerned about what?" a voice asked abruptly.

Melissa and I turned to greet our unexpected guest.

"*Shalom*, my friends."

Rabbi Eli Cohen, realizing that he had caught us off guard, stepped out from behind the corner nearby.

"You think Rabbi Cohen will not be concerned about what?' he pressed a second time, with a pleasantly reassuring expression in his forever-thoughtful eyes.

Melissa looked at me with a reddening face.

"Oh . . ." I hesitated, obviously startled by the unexpected appearance. "Missy's just having a hard time with things."

"I'm sorry," the professor smiled kindly as only he could do. "It is a most difficult hour for all of us. Even so, Sarah and Rebecca are safely on their way to Tel Aviv and my Joseph, so shall we proceed?"

We nodded, then followed the troubled professor past the

guard gate at the university.

Within minutes, the rabbi entered the small office in the Humanities wing of the university library ahead of us. Without speaking further of his son, he placed the ancient records out on top of the table before us.

"The hour of further translating has arrived," he announced triumphantly. "While my colleagues have the first set of scrolls from the news conference, we are free to begin the second phase of our project. The third set of scrolls, as you know, has been placed in the archive safe, and will remain there until we are ready to translate it.

"Incidentally," he continued, glancing over at Melissa, "photographs have been made of all three sets, but they will not be released to the world until our work has been completed. What's more, when you translate, you will use common English when this Mary is speaking . . . other than when she is repeating scripture, of course. Jason and I determined to write this way in translating the first set of scrolls, and it reads clearly."

All of this I knew, but I appreciated his thoroughness in bringing Melissa up to date.

Professor Cohen smiled as though he hadn't a care in the world, then politely offered us the first solid glimpse of the scrolls. Simultaneously glancing down at the beginning of the tattered parchments, we each felt the emotions of the moment come alive inside our hearts. For me, it was breathtaking to once again see the work, and especially to share the ancient Hebraic parchments with the woman who had become my closest friend. Still, my heart saddened as I again realized that I wouldn't be sharing the translating experience with Sid. It didn't seem right that he would leave as he did; but after learning of his proposal, and Melissa's rejection, I could not blame him.

A thought then entered my mind that surprised me. It had nothing to do with Sid or Melissa. I began asking Rabbi Cohen questions that I had not previously considered. "Is Mary Magdala here today? Does she know us? Is she content to have her work transcribed by two Americans? And most of all . . . are we really worthy of the task?"

I hoped so, and from the rabbi's reply, I felt encouraged. Knowing Melissa's declared feelings of unworthiness, it was a most intriguing "connection" to consider.

These thoughts spun into others, and before we knew it, we were wondering aloud what new treasures we would find. Then, without further dialogue, we began the process of translating. As we read from right to left and mouthed the first translated words into English, my eyes were so brimming with tears that I could barely make out the ancient hieroglyphics on the first line. I didn't know if my tears were for Melissa's being there, or for my re-introduction to the ancient Mary. I just knew they were real, and they fell effortlessly into my lap. Melissa was crying also, and although neither of us chose to share with Rabbi Cohen our previous hour's conversation, I could sense the joy within Melissa's heart. *It is a beginning,* I considered. *Clearly, it is a beginning—*

Working out a system of recording the ancient woman's thoughts into the computer, the three of us were soon lost in a sea of ancient Hebraic expressions . . . words written over two thousand years ago by an aging yet articulate Mary of Magdala.

Part Two

THE STORY

MY LORD'S MINISTRY

As Written by Mary of Magdala, and
Entrusted to John Mark
A.D. 68

I

Praise God that life continues to uphold and strengthen me, that I am once more given the light of another day. And glory be to the heavens for my Lord's sake, that I may return again to that sacred calling I feel so urgent inside me to keep the record of his life, and to preserve it with my recorded memory.

While it has been well over thirty years since Jesus' crucifixion and departure, still the recollection of that conflicting hour of miracles continues to subdue my heart. I cannot fully say why I continue to feel exposed, but I know it is an emotion that can only be salved by once again feeling my Lord's presence. For now, however, I know that there is a purpose in writing of my remarkable friend from Nazareth—my Lord Jesus. Even now, through the sorrow of tears long since shed, my heart leaps for joy at the sound of his name. My soul is soothed by his love, for it continues to burn deep inside me.

I questioned once, shall it always be so? Shall the glory of my Lord's strength as a resurrected being fill me forever with such wonder? I believe that it shall, for I am consumed with a strength beyond my own, simply contemplating the thought. After all, I know that he is from everlasting to everlasting. My doubts come only when I consider my failures and inadequacies as one loved by the Holy One of Israel. For I too am sometimes blinded and beguiled by the craftiness of the Adversary. He offers complacency and idleness, and I am at times encumbered by both. After all, I could—and should—be doing so much more for those who suffer.

Jesus did. He gave himself always to others. He never failed to be there for someone, even when they did not deserve to be with him. He healed the lepers, he caused the lame to walk and the deaf to hear. He opened the eyes of the blind, and even brought forth the dead from their graves. He amazed all who witnessed his miracle-making, and set them to wonder who he really was. Nevertheless, I have learned that it is by the truth and power of his words that I have come to know him as my personal Lord.

That is who he is!

Sometimes I wonder if he will forgive me for having to be released of seven evil spirits, or devils. How I wish I had not made myself vulnerable to them in the first place. Still, in my heart, I feel that he already has forgiven me for my infirmities. Perhaps this is why I continue to chronicle his experiences among the living—his ways and his message to the world on these parchments of leather.

It is odd, really. I cannot seem to find rest on a given day, unless I have written a thought or an act of his as I remember it. Yet, when I do record my recollections, when I search my mind for the glorious memories that lie within, I find not only a restful reprieve, but a continuously more edifying lift to my often-troubled soul. I am comforted when I write, and I am troubled when I do not. Mere words seem void of expressing the grandeur of his glory, so instead, I search my heart for feelings. I then try, with humility of might and soul, to paint a picture with my words. I can only pray that he will accept them as my personal testament to his greatness.

Perhaps if I continue to tell his story, rather than my own, I will no longer feel the guilt of my omissions. Instead, in all likelihood I will be once again lifted upon the wings of his mercy. It is my feeling that someone in the future—perhaps even one who translates my words—will need to know of my weaknesses. To that person I offer hope—my Savior's hope.

I am Mary of Magdala, daughter of Lamech, and this second set of parchments contains the work of my very own fingers. They are my thoughts, my feelings, and my memories—inscribed herein to benefit generations yet unborn. They are manifestations of my loyalty to Jesus Christ . . . my Lord and my God.

I knew him well. I have said this often—in fact, ever since I met him on our way to Jerusalem when we were both in our thirteenth year. From that day forward, I found myself richly blessed by our association. He was a friend of incomparable goodness, for he imparted truths of lasting, noble worth to me. His very presence enlightened me, as it did our friends, and his warmth and personal care gave me hope that, to this day, is my well spring for life.

There is a wondrous joy in this Jesus. Even today, after three decades since his departure, my heart cries out with gladness—for he is unquestionably and unwaveringly still there. On this morning I shall begin to record his ministry in the flesh, for so the Holy Spirit prompts.

Today is a beautiful day here upon the hills of Galilee. I have come to a high and quiet place—almost half way between my home village of Magdala and the seaport village of Capernaum. After all, these were the places where I would sit and learn from my Master. Here, in the comfortable shadows of large trees shading a small meadow near the summit of Mt. Tabor, I quietly and reverently relive his life anew.

I come here often, filled with hope for the things I have both heard and remembered. The sights around me are familiar ones—the birds singing, the trees rustling in the breeze, the waves of grass serenading in their movement, and the warmth of the sun glistening out across the Sea of Galilee. Nazareth, my Lord's mountain village but an hour's journey to the south, forever reminds me of the sublime moments my friends and I shared with Jesus. These are all familiar sights to me now, just as they were to him while he was yet with us, gracing us with his presence. Oh, that the heavens could again be so generous—for truly, those were extraordinary days for those who had accepted him.

I miss him so.

There are times when I still see his eyes smiling warmly piercing my very soul. I also see his generous outstretched hands offering comfort to me when in need.

Tears come easily for me. Nevertheless, I am not ashamed of them, for they speak the language of my soul. They are not tears of sadness or of grief, but are manifestations of gratitude and humility from one who considers serving my Savior to be the most precious gift of all.

Nor is Jesus within the Garden Tomb. He is risen, and dwells with the Father of us all! Yet still his spirit lingers, providing comfort to all who believe in his name. It is as though he continues to walk the earth, surrounding each of his followers with a light that never dims.

Through the Comforter, I *feel* him. I know that he is here. We are his flock, and his love for us is without condition. That is why he does not turn his back on us. He now resides as a Supreme Being, and he took his seat at the right-hand side of the Father. There he watches, whispers, and cares for us, even as we continue to seek him. His understanding of each individual is truly remarkable. He knows all of us, even by name.

It is true. I marvel at his memory. Yea, his ability to remember each person, and each person's heart, was nothing less than divine. As I reflect upon the events where so many of my friends and neighbors were present, I remain inspired that he knew each of them, and not only by name. For in truth, he has *always* known them.

Nonetheless, this is not the greatest of his miracles, for no miracle could compare with the rising of his own flesh from the unfinished tomb.

Many ask, how can this be? The Roman soldiers were foolish to think that they could rid the world of him so quickly, so easily! He did not die at their hands, but by his remarkable will alone did he make the decision to pass into the world beyond our own.

He suffered. Oh, how he suffered . . . bleeding from every pore. He gave up his life so that we might live again, because he had agreed to do so for the salvation of our souls. For behold I know that each and every one of us who has lived in mortality will, because of him, have the opportunity to obtain his greatest gift of all—salvation!

Salvation. I am humbled by this generous blessing. Salvation. That is what he called it. "The salvation of our immortal souls." Understanding this truth as little as I do, I cannot help but wonder if I will ever feel totally worthy of so great a gift.

Jesus was no ordinary man. He told me once that life itself was nothing more than a proving ground for all of Father's children. He said that each of us, while dwelling in a pre-mortal sphere, elected to come here to the earth—*his* earth—to choose our own destiny.

His words, so often spoken with tenderness and emotion, soothed my soul like the healing oils of the physicians. His directions were accurate, and his love was complete.

He loved us individually; and I have, and always *will*, love him—

A Season in Which to Prepare

II

Shortly after my family moved from the Galilee seaside village of Magdala, to our mountainous home in Nazareth, my father took work with the stone masons. Once there, I was given the hoped-for experience of reuniting with my friends, Mary and Martha, with their brother Lazarus, and of course with Jesus.

By this time, Jesus had grown into an exceedingly handsome man, and had mastered the building skills of his earthly father, Joseph. His talents with wood were unlike any I had ever before seen. For years, he had built furniture and other fine objects with his father's direction, and had refined his craft with such success that people far and wide sought his handcrafted treasures. And yes, this is a subject for thought on its own. Jesus needed to provide for himself and his family, it was true. Even so, he gave any excess to needy friends and strangers who had somehow been fortunate enough to pass his father's workshop. He never once allowed himself to be adorned with riches. For lo, he would not have it. He gave always what he did not need, and seemed to always sacrifice his own comforts for the comforts of those who were less fortunate.

"`Tis easier for a camel to pass through the eye of a needle," he once said, "than for a rich man to get into heaven."

So he worked hard, keeping a humble, sacrificing lifestyle that eventually served a small multitude of well-deserving people in need. Jesus, of course, seemed to grow just a little taller from each of these experiences, for he smiled serenely after the passing of each and every gift.

Lazarus, Mary, and Martha had moved with their parents to Nazareth, where Jesus lived, long before my family determined to do the same. The three of them, with Jesus as their pivotal friend, had become inseparable. Together, they studied in the synagogues, worked with their families in the village shops, and assisted one another in all things. More importantly, they became unified in the faith, growing spiritually by following the example of the Master, even prior to his formal ministry.

Adhering to Jewish tradition, Jesus did not officially embark on his singular season of public service until he had reached an adult age of thirty years. Even so, before that time he never missed an opportunity to teach us about the wonders of the heavens. And we could not help but marvel!

When I joined my friends in Jesus' village several years after we first met, I was immediately encircled by their love and affection. Truly, I felt like I had always been there with them, even as I had been with them at the Passover. Of a truth, Jesus seemed pleased to have me nearby.

I once took a walk with Jesus following the celebration of his nineteenth birthday. There was a small, but well-worn path that led away from our village and wound its way to the top of the overlook upon which I presently sit. From here, we could see the dimly silhouetted shadows of the structures below us in the village. An occasional animal, moving slowly about, would remind us of who we were, and how we fit into our little hillside home. A fresh-scented evening with color filling the skies lingered overhead. In the air, the birds sang and fluttered about from one olive or locust tree to the next.

As the day gave way to night, I saw a certain look in Jesus' eyes that left me curious. I supposed that there was something beyond my sight, for he was looking up into the heavens and softly whispering words I could not understand. As he spoke, tears brimmed his eyelids, then fell unrestrained downward over his cheeks.

"Are you alright?" I asked, wondering if he was thinking of something of concern.

"I am fine," he rejoined calmly, moving no other muscles than those surrounding his mouth.

"What is it then, my Lord?"

"The firmament."

"The fir . . . firmament?"

"Yes, Mary," he whispered quietly, "the firmament. Do you understand the meaning of the word?"

Speaking plainly, I replied that unfortunately I did not.

"It means the vastness of heaven, Mary. It is a single word that is used to describe all that we see from our home here on earth. The stars, the moon, the other worlds in the galaxies above—all are part of the firmament of heaven."

"It sounds beautiful!" I exclaimed, my mind suddenly alive in searching.

Continuing, he asked, "Did you know that this endless beauty above us here tonight is the same splendor afforded to your first mortal parents so long ago?"

"My first mortal parents, Jesus?" I pressed, not quite sure what he was trying to tell me.

"Yes, Mary," he answered calmly, "Adam and Eve. They were together in the Garden of Eden, you know, four millennia ago. They saw, even as we see this evening, the same glorious firmament."

The idea was enthralling. It made me feel like a little girl again; at the foot of my mother, listening with wonder to the words of her bedtime stories. For me, the idea of Adam and Eve having been here on the earth so long ago was difficult to comprehend. It was more like a tale told best in the circles of the wise. Yet, the more I spent time with Jesus, listening to his words, the more clear my image became of my first parents. Somehow I sensed that Jesus knew them well. A thousand years—or even four—did not seem to blur his memory.

They really had lived here on the earth, even as I did. They really had been my first mortal forebearers, and really did provide the means for me to come here to the earth. And now, here was a thought with a unique image of its own. Being inquisitive, they had undoubtedly looked up into the heavens on a night like this, had seen the same firmament and all its beauty just as we were seeing. In so doing, their spirits had likely been lifted, even as we had experienced lift to *our* souls this night. We were very possibly seeing the same stars. It was a feeling of extraordinary peace from which I found a great deal of unexpected comfort.

"Hmmm . . ." I thought aloud, gazing again into the light of the endless stars above me, while at the same time glancing over at my Lord, "these are the visions of eternity!"

Jesus looked at me and smiled.

"They are what you have declared them, Mary," he replied compassionately. "They are visions of eternity."

For several quiet moments, Jesus scanned the heavens above, focusing his attention on specific parts of the sky. I was content just to be sitting there with him in the shadows of the night, but even more so after having witnessed his warm and affectionate smile. I followed, as best I could, every star I perceived him to see, and inwardly wished that I had the all-seeing, penetrating faculties of vision that were his.

"Do you see it, Mary?" he asked suddenly, disturbing the

silence.

I glanced upward once more, trying to focus on the general direction Jesus had referred me to, then squinted slightly in order for my eyes to adjust.

"See what?" I inquired, keeping my gaze heavenward, but glancing over at my Lord for better clarification and direction.

"That star," Jesus spoke softly, pointing towards the northern skies.

"Star?" I inquired honestly. "What star? I see millions of stars, Jesus."

My Lord continued to stare for a moment longer, into the expanse of the firmament. Of a truth, he did not seem to notice that I was struggling to see what had so attracted him. He had a far-away look in his eyes as if to suggest that he had seen this particular star at some other moment in time, and was currently remembering the same. But there was also a measure of longing in his piercing blue eyes, as well . . . a longing for something unseen. I thought that perhaps it was a star that brought light to his world . . . to Heavenly Father's world. Perhaps it was the place he had referred to as heaven.

"What do you see, Jesus?" I inquired softly.

"There," he exclaimed, pointing with his right index finger, "close to that star in the northern sky, is where I dwelt with the Father."

Trying to understand, I looked longingly toward where he was pointing. "That one, my Lord?"

"Yes, Mary . . . that very one."

"You *lived* there?"

"I did," he rejoined thoughtfully.

"Where . . . is it?"

"It was there that I lived with the Father while creating this earth."

I looked at him searchingly. "Our earth? You mean *you* made this world?"

"Under the Father's direction."

For a moment, I was overwhelmed by my Lord's claim. Perhaps I had taken for granted some of the knowledge that had been given unto me in my early life. For I had learned, years earlier, that Jesus had been the Creator of the earth. I was astonished to think that here, sitting beside me, was the very God of that creation process. As the prophet Jeremiah had written, I was born spiritually like everyone else, long before the world was created. And, like all others, I was brought to the earth to prove myself worthy to return to the Father's presence. Nevertheless, before I came to the world, Jesus had already worked with Father in the creation process. By his hands, this very world had been created. And here was I . . . a simple soul, seated and in conversation with the Creator, himself!

"This is Father's footstool," Jesus said suddenly. "It is a special world, unique in the firmament. It is sacred to him."

"But . . . why?"

"Because," he said, a tear suddenly forming in the corner of his eye, "this is the earth that the Father chose for me. I came here to receive my own body of flesh and bone. I came here to suffer . . . and of course to die."

"What?" I countered anxiously, "Die? What are you talking about, Jesus?"

My Lord did not feel the time to be right to tell me about the suffering he would later be called upon to endure. But he did say these words, fixed like granite in my memory: "Like all of the sons and daughters of man, I too will give up my mortal body at the moment of my death, and rise to the heavens as a spirit."

I did not understand then what I do now; that he would do far more than this. I could not comprehend the agony that would eventually be his. Nor could I begin to understand the mission that he had been called upon to perform here in mortality.

And now I must once again stop my writing. Hebraic expressions consume so much time and space, but it is the only language that I know. Would that I had learned Egyptian, the scribal language that can speak much in such an abbreviated manner. But I will write more following the Sabbath, when my mind and fingers have enjoyed their day of rest. On the morrow I will observe my Lord's day, remembering him as I remember my covenants to the Father—the promises I made in the River Jordan so many years ago.

My Lord's Forerunner

III

The preparations Jesus made were deeply engaging. He understood the need for personal obedience to all of the edicts of the Father, and he never wavered in attempts to fulfill everything asked of him. His youthful intellect was coupled with spirituality. This allowed him to see deeply into the mission that was his long before he set about the task appointed him.

My Lord was blessed with a family who loved him dearly. His mother was an angel sent from a beautiful court in the heavens by God, himself. She was so beautiful and kind. Her temperament was gracious and her mannerisms were delicate and friendly. Joseph, Mary's husband, was likewise gentle-hearted, while uncompromising and firm. Leaving nothing to chance, he somehow knew the earthly stewardship that was his, and he instilled integrity and honor in the hearts of all of his children.

Jesus was an admirable eldest child. Even in his youth, he gave new meaning to the practice of being kind to his younger siblings. Nor did they oppose his forthright though righteous authority over them. Instead, they hung on his every word, relying upon him to choose the right course for them to follow.

In time, a great number of people in and around our village

began seeking the companionship of my Lord. Cousins, friends, and enemies alike took a peculiar interest in him. He associated with each of them, trying as only he could, to instill righteousness in their hearts. The more the people knew him, the more they desired to be close to him. Our village became a place of adulation and curiosity as the word of this worker of miracles spread throughout the land.

One afternoon while Jesus, Mary, Lazarus, and I were walking down through the streets of Nazareth, we were suddenly besieged by a storm that, in my few years on the earth, I had never before encountered. Those who had thronged about us, eager to catch a momentary glimpse of the Savior, or to perhaps touch the hem of his garment, quickly scattered to places of safety.

The winds picked up to a great speed while rain and thunderous pelting from the skies showered down upon us like an angry beast. I remember the lightning most of all, and thought about taking refuge under a tile roof nearby.

"We must shelter ourselves!" I exclaimed, hoping that Jesus would lead us to where I was pointing. But Jesus did not come. Instead, as the rest of us gathered under the protective cover, Jesus stood out in the rain and allowed the winds and the deluge to grind away at him with all its fury. There was, on the Master's face, a picture of calm that I had never before seen. It was as though he had expected this storm to come; and now that it had, his countenance was blithe and serene.

"Jesus," Lazarus cried out, "you must come hither! There is shelter here! We must protect ourselves!"

But Jesus did not respond. Instead, he continued to stand there, gazing heavenward. Passers by went quickly to their shelters, and the rains intensified. Some of the younger children were heard shrieking and crying as the storm's furious toll became a part of the scenery around us.

"By the heavens," Lazarus shouted a second time, clearly more concerned with every passing minute, "What has brought this terrible tempest upon us?"

To the right, a wooden structure was lifted from its foundations. The site was horrifying, for there were those inside whose welfare had depended upon its protection.

"Jesus!" Mary called out. "Help them, Jesus!"

Nevertheless, Jesus still did not so much as acknowledge that we were calling after him.

"Oh, dear Lord," I began to cry, wondering all the while whether the storm would tear away at the building under which we were standing as well. "What manner of madness is this? From whence hath this storm come?"

The family of the single dwelling that had been ripped from its foundation had escaped miraculously to a neighbor's home. But a young child, an infant, had been struck in the head by an object unknown to me, and was losing blood.

"Dear heavens, no!" I slapped a hand over my mouth, for I could not bear the sight of the little one's injury. Nevertheless, I was glad that the others had escaped. I was frozen with fear as I continued to monitor the intensity of the storm. It was unnerving. I believed that I would see the entire village disappear in its fury. And then many would die.

I thought again about the young child I had seen. I wondered if he was badly hit, or if his life might be in peril. Why hadn't Jesus taken a special interest in the boy? It just didn't seem right. The storm was like a devil to me. Its power was not from this world. I did not know why I thought thus, but there seemed to be something dreadful connected with it. For, as the rains turned to hail and the winds intensified, I watched bewildered as my Master stood undaunted in the street, seemingly unconcerned and untouched by the fast-falling ice-rains from the skies. It was as though the storm could not harm my Lord, for he stood within the boundaries of its furious assault like a paladin of stone.

"Jesus!" we called out to him several times. But never once did he respond. Instead, he kept a vigilant watch on the far end of the city . . . as if expecting something, or someone.

Then, at last, a shadow emerged in the distance. A stranger came into full view; standing as the Savior stood, out in the center of the long, narrow street. He too had been traveling with a flock of followers from afar . . . multitudes of people we had never before seen. These people, abandoning their apparent leader, sought refuge in diverse places throughout the village.

At last the stranger himself stood alone in the streets, facing from a distance, the gaze of Jesus.

"They are fools!" I heard a nearby villager uttering to another.

"They shall perish!" another yelled out.

I cast my eyes briefly at the place where they stood, then turned to once again behold my Lord. I knew that they were not fools. I also knew—though I did not understand why—that neither would be hurt by the terrible tempest.

Lazarus tapped me upon the shoulder "Who is that?" he whispered. "Who cometh nigh, at the time of this great and formidable storm to greet the Master?"

"I know not," I breathed honestly.

Then, as we huddled together watching, waiting, we saw a miraculous thing—

Abruptly, another string of lightning discharged downward from the skies and visually engulfed the figure at the far end of the street. He was but a small speck to our vision, but it was clear that the brightness had encircled him like a fiery furnace.

Nevertheless, he did not appear to be hurt, but stood like a soldier, unwavering.

Jesus began to walk slowly toward the stranger, even as the man approached Jesus.

Another finger of lightning from the heavens suddenly flashed and illuminated them both. The stranger did not seem afraid, but walked calmly forward. My friends and I were astonished. In our hearts, we saw a pending tragedy, and wished again that our Lord would join us under the protective cover of the overhang.

"Who is that?" I called out to the Master, but it was as if he could not hear me.

"Jesus?"

For a moment, there was only silence and the motions of the turbulent sky overhead. Then—

"My friends," the Lord at last spake, "behold, my cousin, John."

We could do no more than watch and wonder. To us the experience had been terrifying. We had thought that both Jesus and his cousin would eventually be slain by the heavenly tumult, but it had not been so. Instead, a ring of fire circled about them, as if to suggest that they were supposed to meet in this unusual way. Perhaps we were to be witness to the great wonders from the skies, and perhaps it was our destiny to take note of this event for some purpose known only to God. We did not know. Nevertheless, when the raging deluge had passed, there was a reunion of two endearing souls who held each other tightly, and our hearts leapt for joy at their coming together.

Behind us, huddled under the roof of a neighbor's home, the young child who had been hit in the head during the storm cradled in his mother's arms and met her eyes with his own. He had been weeping from the pain, and could not be consoled. Then suddenly, his crying ceased. I had taken a special interest in the boy and had hoped that my Lord would do the same. Nonetheless, I had supposed that he had not, for he had not turned to pay heed to the cries of the child. Instead, Jesus had pressed forward to meet his cousin and had seemingly turned a deaf ear to the young boy's plight.

Jesus, however, did not turn a deaf ear to any child! For, as the storm passed, so also passed the screams of the little one. His wounds were no longer visible, and his weeping had turned to a quiet whimper. The baby had been healed in that same moment, leaving each of us to once again ponder the wonder of my Lord's power.

I cried, but said nothing. With my own eyes, I had seen the deep wound in the young child's face, and now I saw only the flesh of a healthy baby son. The others had seen also, and when the mother of the child realized what had happened, she turned to Jesus and wept.

She knew. She knew who he was, and she fell down and worshiped him.

Very much like Jesus, himself, his cousin John became an integral part of the Lord's transcendent season of service. I will now speak of him.

John was born six months earlier than Jesus; and, according to the Savior, John had been selected by the Father to prepare the way for the Messiah.

Like Mary, the mother of Jesus, Zacharias had also received a glorifying angelic visitation, announcing Elizabeth's pregnancy with John. God, in his wisdom, had determined to bring forth a prophet to this land. It was the first time in more than four hundred years that a prophet had been among my people, and it was right that he now be upon the earth.

John was a popular man. He was an exceedingly influential tutor whose mission, I later understood, was to preach repentance unto the children of men. He was to prepare as many as would listen, to be baptized and to take upon themselves the name of Jesus Christ. Many came into the kingdom through John. Many, I trust, will be saved in the eternal worlds of the Father because of his perseverance.

John's influence was engendered by an enlightened mind which, like unto my Lord, understood the truths of the Father. But there was much more to John than this. He had within him the powerful influence of the Holy Spirit. He had an important message to impart, and did not hesitate to warn others of the need to repent.

"Come unto Jehovah!" he exclaimed on one occasion. "He is the Holy One . . . the Lamb of God. He will come after me, and with mightier power."

Within six months of John's ministry, he had aroused the curiosity of the leaders of the entire Jewish nation. Many believed that it was he who had been foretold of by the earlier ancients—that he, John the Baptist, was the long awaited Messiah. But, he was *not* the Messiah! Instead, just as he had spoken, he was a heralder for the Messiah.

The Baptist spoke boldly against the evil wrong doers of the people, and even challenged the mighty Herod Antipas, our country's king and ruler. He condemned others as he announced what would come to pass if they should continue to serve the devil. Their souls he placed on probation, and he challenged them fearlessly that they should change their hearts before it was too late. This he did because of their incestuous and adulterous marriages. He proclaimed, without trepidation, the imminent arrival of the Messiah, taking no thought for his own life or safety from the butchering Romans. In the end, it was said among my people that "John did no miracle; but all things that John spake of this man, Jesus, were true."

I was always so grateful for the honorable words Jesus spoke in John's behalf, for never was there a doubt in the minds of those who would listen, that Jesus loved and admired his blessed prophet/cousin.

On one occasion, King Herod confined John to a dungeon. While he was there, my Lord graciously called upon the heavens themselves to provide the weary Baptist with a measure of comfort. The event was nothing less than divinely orchestrated.

Angels came and ministered unto John . . . angels from heaven!

I have given much thought to this happening, and to the spiritual might of John the Baptist. In order for him to fulfill the divinely designated role as witness of the Messiah, careful pre-earthly considerations had to have been made by the Father and the Son.

John was of the lineage of Aaron. This ancestral line was essential, for without it he would not have been entitled to priesthood power. Jesus once told me that John had a pre-earth appointment as a prophet, and had been ordained to that purpose in a Grand Council of heaven before the world was.

There was a sign given—

John the Baptist was like unto Jesus, for when his father, Zacharias, was visited by the angel Gabriel nearly a year before John's birth, he had been struck dumb. All of those who knew Zacharias, knew also that he *had* seen an angel. The people acknowledged also that Zacharias had been struck dumb, and many were fearful lest they too might suffer the same fate.

As they beheld the open powers of the heavens manifest themselves through this miracle, many who did not believe, were given to know the truth when at last the voice of Zacharias was restored to him. And many marveled at this son of the stricken man. John. John the prophet. John the Baptist. John, the child of promise.

There was an afternoon, long ago, that I remember vividly. My Lord and I were traveling near the banks of the Jordan River where great multitudes of people had gathered to hear and to take part in John's teachings. Many, we witnessed, appeared to recognize the resplendence of the prophet, for there were great numbers from both Judea and Jerusalem who went out to meet him. From regions all around Jordan they came, confessing their sins while entering the waters of baptism. Many, even publicans and soldiers, had come to seek John's word.

I marveled at this.

Not long after this incident, when my Lord was preparing for his ministry in northern Galilee, he made a bewildering declaration. He privately revealed his need to enter the waters of baptism, and likewise be baptized.

"What meanest thou?" I asked of him, knowing full well that Jesus could not have need of baptism according to my understanding. For I understood that this sacred ordinance was designed for the purpose of the sinner and the repentant. Jesus, as far as I knew, had done nothing for which to repent, yet he insisted that his time for immersion had arrived.

Again I inquired as to whether I had properly learned the meaning of this ordinance for my Lord, and asked him why *he* should submit to baptism.

"That others might understand," he said plainly unto me, "and therefore follow after me in the path of righteousness. It is ordained unto all of Father's children to be so immersed."

Follow after him? I then understood.

It was clear that Jesus had decided that tutoring by example would be the greatest medium of enlightening those who might not otherwise understand. I had heard about John's baptisms, but until that very moment had not really given the thought that I now knew it deserved. The notion led me to believe that I too should follow after him. I wanted to be baptized, and this feeling in my heart brought a renewed measure of hope.

Jesus crossed over to the Jordan River, seeking out his cousin, John. As Matthew later shared with me, the Savior's singular moment of baptism—and of a marvelous heavenly manifestation—took place in solitude.

"Good morning, dear cousin," Jesus called enthusiastically, even as he descended toward the water's edge.

"Salutations, my Lord."

The robust, red-bearded John stabbed his staff into the dirt, stopped short, and grinned. "It has been too long, cousin," he enthused, bowing humbly before my Lord. "For what purpose has thou sought me here upon the banks of the mighty Jordan?"

"That thou mightest baptize me," Jesus answered softly.

"But, my Lord," John protested innocently, "I have need to be baptized of *thee,* and comest thou to me?"

"Of a surety, dear cousin."

Jesus' response was spoken with deftness, but with a gentleness that gave birth to an even deeper breadth of emotions from John. "Suffer it to be so now; for thus it becometh us to fulfill all righteousness."

Without further conversation, Jesus lifted the hem of his garment and descended into the swirling inlet. "Come, John . . . it is time."

John hesitated only briefly. Then, with a prayer of gratitude, he entered the water where Jesus was standing. Communicating eye-to-eye and heart-to-heart, he raised his right hand and began: "Jesus of Nazareth, having been commissioned of thee, I baptize thee in the name of the Father, and of Thee, and of the Holy Ghost. Amen."

John slowly lowered the Savior of the World into the water surrounding them. Once submerged, Jesus came up straightway out of the river. Looking into the heavens, both John and Jesus were taken back as the Spirit of God—the third member of the godhead—descended just as a dove would descend, and lighted upon my Lord.

Simultaneous to the arrival of the Holy Spirit, God the Father—the very sire of him to whom the world owed its very existence—spoke: *"This is my Beloved Son, in whom I am well pleased."*

This pronouncement of fatherhood brought tears of joy—both to Jesus and to John. Each was increasingly aware of the profoundness of the moment, and the manifestation of the other two members of the Godhead. For John, this was the crowning moment of his life, and he bowed his head in reverence. He had witnessed the vocal announcement of the very God to whom he offered his oblations. What's more, he had visually gained testimony of the Spirit of all Truth. Christ—the man/god whose flesh was his flesh—had begun his earthly ministry. For John, the forerunner, it was a singular moment in all the eternities.

As Jesus later taught me, John's personal experience with all three members of the Godhead made him one of the world's most able witnesses. It is little wonder that the devil sought to destroy him early. Indeed, it still saddens my heart to recall John's cruel and unnecessary death at the hands of the corrupt. But, recall it I must.

Several months following the advent of my Lord's baptism, the wicked Herod Antipas imprisoned John, then tortured and scourged him with a cat-of-nine tails. Even more dreadful was John's ultimate execution. The evil shadow in the heart of Antipas had grown stronger prior to that dark hour. Because of his inability to bridle his passions, Antipas had allowed a young woman—the dancing girl, Salome—to entice him to murder!

John, our beloved prophet and friend, was beheaded at the order of Herod.

Oh, that I could let this part of John's life rest . . . that I could be spared the turmoil of this memory. But I cannot. I must write this chapter of his life as it deals directly with my Lord's history, and I am left to deal with the despair of that memory.

Herodias, the estranged wife of Antipas, had schemed with the dancing girl to kill John, and the woman's wicked plan had disturbingly enough worked. I think she was bewitched by a devil, for John was no threat to the king *or* his family.

Oh, how my heart cried out to God on that awful night! I can still feel the consuming sorrow that overshadowed us—for when John was murdered, we wept in bitter bereavement. Even now, it is only John's ultimate hope for a complete resurrection that gives my soul respite. For as I think of that loathsome moment, my mind is consumed by the pain that it knew on that occasion and the tears flow freely still.

I miss John so.

Even now, as I continue to write the words of my heart, I grow weary of the task appointed unto me. It is not always easy to record painful memories, but I do not seek another errand. For now, I put down my marker for the night. What I have spoken is true. I go now to a place of quiet solitude. There I will rest my mortal frame, satisfied in knowing that my Master will agree with the words I have written this day. I am Mary from Magdala, and for the moment, I make an end to these sayings.

On the Slopes of Mount Scopus Overlooking Old Jerusalem

November 7, 1995

IV

The Holy Land.

The name, itself, breathed a hallowedness into my lungs as I lay gazing up into the early evening sky overhead. I was above the traditional Garden of Gethsemane, near the rock entryway and gate of a place known as the Orson Hyde Memorial.

As I adjusted my knapsack as a pillow, I pondered the final words of the ancient Mary's writings, and again wondered if she was aware that Melissa and I were working on her parchments. That we were the ones to whom these records had been entrusted was almost more than my mind could concede. Somehow, the thought of such a stewardship brought a sense of reverence—as well as a wonderful peace—to my soul.

We had worked on the text long into the afternoon. The work was tedious, to be sure, but was well worth the time it had taken. While Melissa returned to her dorm, I came here to the slopes of the Mount of Olives to catch a glimpse of the stars in the eastern skies. I had wanted to be alone, to reflect on the words of Mary. I also wanted to offer up a personal prayer that I felt was long overdue.

Little Joseph Cohen was still suffering. He had not pulled free from the coma as we had expected, but was still quite alone at the hospital in Tel Aviv.

I thought about the boy's family—Professor Cohen, Sarah, and of course his younger sister, Rebecca. I thought about Joseph's bravery. What had prompted him to shield Rebecca from the flying bullets? What had given him the courage to act rather than to merely react?

There were other issues, as well—

Melissa had been on my mind. I didn't understand it, but I was becoming increasingly lonely. I had spent the entire week shoulder-to-shoulder with her, and had shared everything with her. At times, when our minds meshed together on a specific portion of the scrolls, I would see Melissa out of the corner of my eye and feel her warmth and comradery. I would also feel her appreciation for me, as well as her love. I needed her. Indeed, I desired to be with her more with every passing day. Even with her troubled spirit—or perhaps *because* of it—I wanted to never leave her side.

Was it all in my head?

The writings of the first manuscript were poignant and revealing. Mary, from Magdala, had done her job well. She had painted a picture of the Savior of the world like nothing I had ever read. That picture was now under review. With Sid disappearing back to the states, Melissa and I were undertaking a project of immense proportions. Though we were often placated by Mary's gentle transcriptions, we knew that the words she spoke were true.

We were translating the words of a woman-friend of the Savior—a contemporary to the Son of God. It was a remarkable experience. Sometimes I would think of myself as being there with Mary; but then the pain of the present would then cause my heart renewed despair. I simply could not clear the events of the past few days from my mind. I could not help but think of the suffering that was taking place in the home of my friends, the Cohens. Nor could I clear my mind of Melissa's own sufferings—demons that had haunted her since she was a little girl. It just wasn't fair.

What would become of my little Israeli friend, Joseph? Would he recover? Would there ever be a time when we would laugh together as we had done so many times before? The medical reports said very little. Still, Joseph was in the care of Israel's finest physicians. More importantly, he was in the capable and caring hands of the Lord.

It had been forty-two long months since I had lost my first wife, Kirsten, to cancer. My personal struggle had been almost more than I was able to endure. But I *had* endured. In fact, I had done more than merely cope. I had experienced a new hope while in Jerusalem, especially since beginning my work on the translation of the Magdalene Scrolls. Because of these writings, my eyes had opened to a very real and distinct truth—Jesus Christ had been a living, breathing human being with a divine Father, and performed a mission of eternal consequence. Through Jesus the doors to eternity had been forever opened, and for those who chose to believe his ascendancy, there was a hope for repentance and happiness. There was also a chance to be healed in mind, body, and spirit.

The healing of the body. That was the operative expression. Through the power of God, young Joseph could be healed completely if we, who loved him, believed. This thought kept swimming through my mind. Joseph was very much in the hands of God, and this thought, alone, provided me a level of comfort. My only hope was that somehow, to some degree, Rabbi Cohen and his family would also come to know that same comfort.

As the hours passed on this particular early evening, I thought more and more about Joseph. I wondered if I should approach the good rabbi and advise him to turn his heart to God. Yet somehow, I already knew that he had. Surely the Savior's love, and his blanket of compassion would become operable for him and his family if they would allow it to be so.

While I continued to gaze heavenward, I wondered if perhaps Mary Magdala, or even the Savior himself, had been to the spot where I now sat. I felt a strange kinship to this woman, and tried to envision what she might look like if she were here with me.

As I conjured mental images of Mary, there came instead a delicate vision of my departed wife, Kirsten. She had been so beautiful, and although time had healed most of the wounds of her passing, my heart ached for her still.

"Kirsten," I asked audibly, "can you hear me?" It was strange to hear those words come out of my mouth. In my heart, I knew that she *was* there. I sensed that she was somehow guiding my pen through the difficult process of translation. At the very least, she was *aware*, and was praying for us.

My father had lost his parents in an explosion in the late 1940s. Through the years, I had come to understand something wonderful about the departed souls of this world. If the holy writ was accurate—and I had implicit faith that it was—my grandparents still lived. Their spirits had not perished with their bodies. Even in death, Jesus had confirmed his relationship with them.

On many occasions, my father said that periodically he had continued *to feel* their company—that they had appeared to him in dreams, that they had never abandoned him.

Dad was such a faith-filled man, and I loved him for that.

I looked again to the heavens—

"Kirsten, darling?" I whispered again, seeing in my mind's eye the face I could never forget. "If you can hear me, I have a favor."

I lay there as if waiting for a response.

"Kirsten?"

The name itself sent a flood of wondrous memories through my mind.

"Can you hear me, Kirsten?"

There was no reply, no confirmation that she could or could not hear me. Still, I felt that she was there.

Off in the distance, I held my gaze firmly upon a single star.

I remembered what Jesus had said to Mary on one of those nights she had written about so long ago. He had drawn her attention to a far away star in the heavens and had told her that it was this same star that had been his home before the world was. The thought was suddenly very intriguing, even personal.

As I gazed into the heavens, I saw the image I had hoped for. I saw the indescribable countenance of a familiar woman; not Mary, but Kirsten. As I rubbed away the image of my departed wife in my mind's eye, I somehow knew that she was alive.

"Help me," I called out. "Help me draw upon the powers of heaven at this pain-filled hour. Help me understand how I can offer a spirit of hope to the professor and his family, as well as to Melissa."

In addition to my concerns for Melissa's fragile mental state, I was becoming increasingly troubled by the Cohen family's grief for the comatose Joseph. They were understandably in shock, and I could only hope that their ordeal would soon come to an end.

"Dear God," I petitioned heavenward, "there are so many things troubling me tonight. What shall become of these people? What can Melissa and I do to assist them in their time of sorrow? What can be done for little Joseph? Is he destined to remain forever in the darkness of his present condition? Or, by thy grace, shall he recover and come back to his family that they might be whole again?

"Oh, Father, can't you see their condition?"

My mind suddenly reverted to Melissa, and to the pervading pain she held captive in her heart. Her past was tragic, to be sure; but it was not the end of the world. She had made mistakes, just as everyone made them. Hers were just more visible. But she had made a wise choice by giving the baby up for adoption. She should be rejoicing in the likelihood of the quality of life she so selflessly granted the child. Instead, she was allowing herself to be wracked with pain.

The Savior's atonement—at least as Melissa perceived it—did not apply. This fact bothered me. She had corrected her life course, she had pled for forgiveness, yet still her heart was riddled with guilt and embarrassment.

"Father," I at last continued, "please grant Melissa thy peace. Please give her to know that she is whole before thee, and that she can rejoice in the sacrifice of thy Son, as it pertains to her. Is that too much to ask? And God, let me know of my future with this beautiful lady . . . that is, if indeed we have a future. It is in thy hands."

I was genuinely touched by the thought of God listening to me and actually intervening—both in behalf of the Cohens as well as Melissa—and I found myself marveling at my faith in Him and His son, Jesus. More than ever, I believed that he lived, and I taxed my mind for answers to the questions that had drawn me to the spot on the sacred hillside where I now lay.

I suddenly considered the implications of the powers of faith.

Here was a prerogative that was divinely unique. The more I considered it, the more consumed I was by all I had learned about righteousness. Mary's writings had touched on the subject several times, and as best as I could recollect, so had the scriptures.

Faith—

That was it . . . that was the answer! As sure as I was observing the increasingly visible stars on this night, so too was there a well-defined purpose for which this principle was taught in the writings of old. Faith, the opposite of fear. The state of mind that produced positive expectations, and gave individuals the *hope*, or assurance in Christ, that was available to them.

Faith. It couldn't be that simple. Yet, could it? What else could I do? In addition to the private agony Melissa was experiencing, it would be the collective efforts of all of those who loved Joseph Cohen that would cause the heavens to respond and hear our cries. If Joseph were to recover, and if Melissa and I were going to be able to translate the writings of Mary with any degree of accuracy, we would have to exercise our faith in God.

I was filled with a new sense of hope at the thought of this course of action, and leapt to my feet ready to run up the hill and tell Melissa what personal inspiration I had received through prayer. It would apply to her own condition, as well as to the Cohens. It was the answer!

As I turned toward the gate, I felt a presence—

Squinting into the darkening path was the shadow of a woman. I was startled by the sight, and for the slightest second, I thought that it was my beloved Kirsten.

It wasn't.

I looked into the shadowed face of my visitor and squinted to see through the ever-increasing darkness of the evening. Then I knew—

Kirsten, Melissa, and Mary

V

"Melissa?"

It was her . . . a silent, regal looking Melissa with a skirt that rippled effortlessly in the evening breeze.

A flurry of wind arose in the evening air, sending goose bumps up my spine. The breeze spread chaotically forward, whipping up the loose debris in front of the stone wall at the entrance of the memorial garden. Although my thoughts surrounding the stories unfolding in the Magdalene Scrolls vanished, the thoughts of Melissa's pain, and of Joseph Cohen's continual suffering, did not vanish. Instead, they seemed more pronounced.

The stars appeared to shine a little brighter since Melissa's arrival. Still, there was a small dust cloud that whirled about beside us, and for a moment it surprised me, causing my heart to beat faster.

"I thought I'd find you here," she grinned, at last speaking.

"Hi, Missy," I swallowed, unable to breathe.

"What are you doing down here all alone?"

"Oh, not much really. Just thinking . . . ."

"Thinking?" she questioned, her soft voice sending goose bumps once again up my spine. She stepped over to the rock retaining wall and sat down beside me. "What are you thinking about, Jason Ellis?"

"This, that, and the other. About you, actually."

"About *me*?"

"That's right," I confirmed, smiling a shy boyish smile. "You . . . and well, Joseph."

The mention of the lad's name brought the predictable despair into her eyes. Obviously, she had been thinking of him as well. All of us were!

For the first time since the accident and Sid's departure, Melissa looked at me with an expression that dazed me. I couldn't think of anything to say, so I returned her stare with a curious expression of my own.

"Are you alright?" She asked caringly.

"I am."

"Then what is it, Jason?"

Replying honestly, but limiting my response to the Cohen family plight, rather than to that *and* Melissa, I said, "It's Joseph. I'm worried about him, as well as his family. I can't help but think that we can help him if we are willing."

"Willing?"

"Yes, Missy," I enthused. "The rabbi hasn't been the same since his son was hit by the sniper's bullet . . . ."

"I know that. But what more can *we* do? He wants us here translating, rather than in Tel Aviv, at the hospital."

"He needs our faith."

"Our faith?"

"That's right," I continued, hoping that she, of all persons would understand. "The boy was brave. He took a bullet for his sister."

"I know."

"Listen to me, Missy. There *is* something we can do for him, for the Cohens."

"And what is that, Jason? The boy is in a coma—"

"We can have faith!"

"Excuse me?"

"You heard me," I pressed. "I'm talking about a collective effort, Melissa. The rabbi isn't *stable.* Not only are his wife and daughter suffering, but he has plummeted into a deep depression. We have to do something. We must call upon the Jesus we've been writing about."

Melissa looked deeply into my eyes, straining to see the urgency that I exuded. "Do you think," she asked, "that our faith will heal him? Joseph, I mean?"

"I do."

"Are you serious?"

"Absolutely."

"You really are, aren't you."

"Of course. I think it's the only way."

Once again, Melissa looked longingly into my eyes. Although she was consumed with her own condition, she too had been worried about the professor's son. In her own mind she had wondered how she could assist the struggling Cohen family. She knew, as I did, that young Joseph was comatose, and that if we did nothing, he would likely remain locked inside this unbearable state for who knew how long—

I could tell that Melissa was touched by my suggestion to exercise our faith in behalf of the Cohen boy. Her eyes narrowed slightly and she gave me a smile that rippled through my body like an electric current.

At last she spoke. "You're a good man, Jason Ellis."

I grinned back.

"Why don't—"

But before her words could come out, a second, oddly robust

dust devil spun out of nowhere and headed straight for us.

"Hold on!" I cried half joking, while watching as the little phenomenon of nature quickly picked up speed. I reached instinctively to put my arms around Melissa and protect her. She didn't seem to mind, and that gave me a strange, reassuring confidence. "Close your eyes!"

"Jason!" she screamed, squeezing her eyelids together as if to suggest that by doing so, the danger would pass. It didn't, of course. Instead, the sudden gust of wind slammed directly into the wall, giving us both a terrific jolt.

Then, as quickly as it had arrived, it vanished.

"Wow!" I exclaimed, still holding Melissa in my arms and trying to get a grip on things. "That was a close call!"

"Close call?" she gasped. "What do you mean *close call?* That wasn't close at all! It was a direct hit!"

"It was incredible," I replied feebly. "Did you see that thing, Missy? I thought it was going to push us right through this wall!"

"Through it?" She looked over at me with searching, disbelieving eyes. "Mmmm . . ." she muttered, at last taking in a deep breath.

"Are you okay?"

I could think of nothing else to say.

For a moment she did not respond. Instead, she remained in my arms like a frightened little girl. I liked the feeling of holding her the way I did beneath the early-evening stars. Even so, I felt an equally persuasive hesitation when the thought of my departed wife came unexpectedly to mind. Was this new emotion alright? Could I put Kirsten into the back of my mind and allow my feelings for Melissa to unfold naturally?

Strangely, I felt that if there was ever a moment of peace for me since things had gone askew, it was now. I felt like a child. I was alive with renewed sensations, and suddenly I felt surprisingly thirsty for Melissa's attention. What's more, although it seemed almost impossible, I sensed that Kirsten *approved.*

In a completely comfortable way, we stood there in each other's arms. Neither of us wanted the moment, and the contact, to end. It was so wonderfully soothing, each of us searching the unspoken thoughts of the other.

Looking up, ever so slowly Melissa's face moved closer. Instinctively I responded, my heart beating out of control. And then our lips met. For a long moment they touched, an urgency building that consumed my emotions.

Something wonderful was taking place—something strange, something unexpected, and something long overdue. With all my heart, I hoped the moment would never end. No longer were my feelings for Melissa competing with those I still treasured for Kirsten. They were two entirely different sets of emotions, and I was delirious. Each of them had their own identity, yet neither crowded the other. But that was way too much to think about at the present. For now, I simply wanted to enjoy the space that was Melissa's; and that's exactly what I did.

We embraced for the longest time, measuring in our own separate ways the magic of the hour. Although for her the embrace had to have implications of healing, I no longer wondered about her feelings for me. Nor did she have to wonder about mine. Again we shared the passion between us by pressing our lips together for a much more romantic expression. When we pulled away for the second time, we knew that we had been longing for one another, yearning for one another. And Melissa? She simply began to cry.

The evening with this wonderful woman was nothing less than magic. Sitting back down, we spent the next hour in each other's arms, discussing everything from our new relationship to little Joseph Cohen's recovery in the hospital. What we did *not* discuss was her unresolved discomfort about her past.

When we finally arose and ambled up the path to our separate dorms, there was an ambience of peace—and love—that would forever change the course of our destinies. Somehow, things would work out. They always did. Melissa would be healed, and the Cohen family would recover.

When at last I climbed into bed, I could not close my eyes. I just lay there rehearsing the extraordinary events of the day. I thought about three very significant women in my life . . . Kirsten, Melissa, and even Mary from the ancient city of Magdala. Each of these women had touched my heart in unique ways, and for reasons I'm not sure I could understand, my eyes blurred over with a film of mollifying moisture.

I was a happy, fulfilled man . . . immensely grateful to my God. Before I closed my eyes for the night, I searched the darkness of my room and once more focused my thinking on that remarkable being of whom Mary had written so much about.

"Thank you," I whispered in the quietude. "Thank you, my Lord."

Pressing forward with the task appointed us, Melissa and I met for breakfast the following morning, then proceeded directly to the university library vault. Barely speaking, each of us basked in the memory of the night before, and the extraordinary scene that had played itself out on Mount Scopus.

At last we found ourselves ready to proceed with our translating. However, Rabbi Cohen was strangely absent, and that worried us. It was not like him. Nor had he left word with the vault assistant. Something did not feel right, and we immediately began to worry. I interrupted our translating several times in order to call the Cohen residence, but there was no answer. Nor had his secretary at the university heard from him. He *had* to be at Joseph's side, in Tel Aviv.

Offering a quiet prayer of hope—and of faith—Melissa and I buried ourselves in the scrolls. He would be in touch. Until then, our progress would keep our minds occupied.

The translating continued—

Forty Days and Forty Nights

VI

My task of scrolling my Lord's ministry is both bitter and sweet. It is bitter in that it causes my heart to once again feel the open wounds of my Lord's suffering. It is also bitter in that I remember mistakes I made in my youth. It is sweet in that my testimony of him, and of his work, increases with each parchment that I complete.

Jesus suffered immeasurably following the slaying of his cousin, John. Following John's death, my Lord began his own ministry with an element of harrowing sorrow. Perhaps it was I alone who interpreted this sadness, but I think not. I do know that, regardless of the pain he experienced in learning of John's execution, my Lord progressed daily with an awareness of his divine mission.

Perhaps it was the absence of his cousin that sent him away from the crowds, away from his friends. For so it was that before Jesus felt ready to impart the truths taught to him by his Father, he left us. Winding down the road toward the Great Sea, he turned south, then ascended to the wilderness of the mountains. His journey took him into the hill-country west of the village of

Jericho—the same area where his cousin, John, had spent so much of his life.

It was in this region that he began to purge himself of any defilements that may have lingered in his heart following John's execution.

I do not say that my Lord had any real reason to rid himself of any evil spirits, for such spirits were never allowed to enter into his perfect soul. Nonetheless, I do believe that he sought his Father's wisdom with a yearning that could only be understood by him. Perhaps it was that he might be healed. It was never given me to know.

Jesus knew that in order to prepare for his ministry, he would ultimately have to take upon himself the pain and suffering of the world. Perhaps not there in the hills and deserts where he sought solitude; but he understood, nevertheless, how dreadfully painful his eventual act of atonement would become.

In the shadows of the treacherous, barren mountains to the south, in a place known only as Qumran, Jesus lived alone for forty days and forty nights. He did not seek to comfort the physical needs of his body, for he fasted all the days of his encampment. He prayed often and sought direction from the angels that ministered unto him. Still, he was subjected to an assault on his spiritual being by Lucifer, his nemesis from the dawn of time.

Some have thought that Jesus went into the wilderness to meet face to face with Satan. I think not. From what he later told me, this extended fast and wilderness sojourn was to draw closer to God, personally. This would have been the natural course of things for Jesus, and makes sense to me; for surely, my Lord would not have purposely sought to interact with, *or* to be tempted of the dark one.

Why should he?

There was clarity in the Savior's eyes the day he left us in

Galilee. It was a need that most of us have felt—a need born of wanting to know our *own* ultimate purpose in life. Jesus wanted to commune with God, his literal Father. Through fasting, and through prayer, he was able to draw close to him.

Nothing could have spiritually prepared my Master more than this time he shared with the Almighty. For after the forty days and nights had passed, Lucifer emerged from the darkness that was his eternal lair, and pressed in upon Jesus with contempt and beguilement. He made every effort possible to tempt the Son of God.

But he could *not!*

Satan understood, perhaps better than any of us, the sacred and unique calling Jesus had received, and utilized all of his given powers to destroy my Lord. After all, was not the chosen Messiah the greatest threat of all to Lucifer's miserable plan?

I cannot repeat all that must have befallen Jesus in that moment of obscurity, for I have only to rely upon the words he spake to me regarding it. What I learned was that the temptations of the adversary were in all aspects vigorous, ruthless, and inexorable.

I know that the devil initially tempted my Lord with food, while Jesus continued to go without. He would not yield. He was like a rock, solid and unwavering in his determination to abstain. He had thought carefully through the temptations that might come to him, and had prepared himself so thoroughly that when at last the temptation did come, he could not be persuaded to fall. That was the God in him.

Satan's cunning was spectacularly orchestrated, however. In tempting the Savior, the most devilish measures would have to be taken to cause his fall from grace. And, oh, how Satan desired Jesus to wither and be slain, that he too might become miserable even as the devil himself. But it would not be! Jesus was the son of God! He was the Master of the universe, and there was no power available to the Lord of Darkness that could seduce him.

Pictures arose in the Savior's mind—pictures of bread and crackers, and of fruits and herbs from the gardens that once seemed abundant behind his home, in Bethlehem. There was everything in its season; the carrots planted and harvested by his mother, the squash also. And the figs in abundance. Everything was there. Everything that Jesus liked. Everything that tasted sweet or savory. Satan showed all these things to my Lord, but food would not bring him down.

So it was that Satan tried something else.

Money. Riches. Earthly riches.

Images of all of the marvelous things that could be acquired by the wealthy were placed in front of Jesus' mind's eye. He was momentarily fascinated by the visions, but once again remained strong in his resolve to overcome this temptation. Great and beautiful works of art and treasures were placed before the Lord's eyes to entice him with all manner of precious things; but he would not yield. When Satan's second attempt became an obvious failure, he again pressed in upon the Lord with something more powerful than even these—

Promises and lies.

Promises were offered by the Lord of Darkness suggesting that Jesus be made a ruler of men, to live a life of ease if he would but renounce the true God of Heaven!

"All these things will I give thee if thou wilt fall down and worship me!" the devil promised abhorrently.

Nevertheless, Jesus did not succumb to these temptations either, for he knew, even then, that Satan was the father of all lies! He knew that Satan could not make him a ruler of men. He knew that Satan could not offer happiness or the serenity of a righteous life. So, he said again, "Get thee behind me, Satan!"

But Satan would not quit—

He accompanied Jesus to a high pinnacle overlooking the still unfinished temple in Jerusalem. It was there that yet another temptation was laid out before the Master. My Lord was told to cast himself down, that no harm would befall him, that angels would bear him up. But this, too, was only partly true. Satan could not have had so great a power to accomplish this thing. Instead, it was the power of the Father, not the devil, that transported my Lord to that high place. One would not fast or seek solitude that he might be accompanied by, or tempted of, the devil!

Jesus went into the wilderness for the purpose of drawing closer to his Father. He sought comfort for his weary soul. He denied his body its physical needs so that his spirit could be nourished by the unique communion with God. When it was over, Jesus came forth with renewed power, and Satan was left powerless.

Jesus had learned obedience through the things which he suffered, and as the beloved apostles would later testify, *"being made perfect, He became the author of eternal salvation unto all them that obey him . . . ."*

So it was that my Lord put on the full armor of God. He then returned to show us all righteousness, and to direct us in his path. There was light in his eyes, and wisdom in his speech. In his countenance there was happiness unlike anything I had known.

Happiness.

He said that, *"Men are that they might know joy."* He wanted me to know that *I* should know joy. He wanted me to tell others the same thing, that the central hope of his Father was that each of us should come to know happiness. It was just that simple. He wanted me to say the word *"Joy!"* Everyone was to learn this precept. Everyone was to eventually understand that happiness was the principal mission of the Savior. Happiness for the children of men.

Oh, how great this message is to me in the twilight of my life. How inspiring! This is the message from the gods! We are not meant to suffer, but to experience peace. We are given to know that it is through our obedience to the laws of God that joy cometh.

Joy at the hands of the Master. Happiness, by *he* who was, and still is, the worker of miracles—Jesus Christ, the son of God!

I chose, on that day, to follow Jesus without restraint. I knew that he was the promised Messiah. I knew that I was a fortunate daughter of God, for it was I who walked with Jesus. It was I who prayed with him, knelt with him, learned from him. From this point forward, I followed no other—

Wondrous Works

VII

I speak now of the more sublime aspects of my Lord's ministry. Herein are the events that clear up any misconceptions of his earthly sojourn. Of a truth, Jesus was no ordinary man. All who knew him were aware of this. All who have read about him understand this. He was the only soul ever to be born whose mother was mortal and whose father was immortal. His Father was God. His Father *is* God. How plain is this truth? God, the father of us all, sired Jesus in mortality. It is true that all of us are the spirit offspring of Heavenly Father, for the prophets have always taught that we were born spiritually before we came to this earth. But we are not like unto Jesus. He was, and is, the son of a *living* God. He is a god!

Jesus understood his divine nature from the beginning. Perhaps, as an infant, he understood less; but clearly he represented the Father all his days. From the time we first attended the Feast of the Passover, Jesus had uncommon understanding . . . godly understanding. He could easily expound upon the plain and precious truths that had been given to him to know. Since I grew up in the same mountainous region near

Jesus' own home, I can say with conviction that there was no other child like him. There were many children whose understanding seemed brilliant to me. Even so, there was no child anywhere who could comprehend—and then expound upon—the things Jesus knew. And why was that?

Where my Lord learned the truths he taught at such an early age was once a mystery to me, though now I am convinced that his Heavenly Father's enlightenment holds the answer. The lessons allotted to him were miraculous tutorials from the heavens, themselves. For though I never knew him to read the sacred Torah, he seemed able to expound upon the scriptures with authority. After all, as Jehovah of yesteryear, he had authored the same. He understood the laws of God with such complete clarity that there remained no man, woman, or child, who could invalidate his teachings. It was as if he knew them as they were written, and he always understood them.

I have supposed that only a God could know that.

He was the child of a miracle. His youthful preparations were portentous, for the early years of his life were stepping stones of self mastery and personal confidence. He did not waiver in these preparations, for he knew that his purpose in mortality would require an exactness of spirit and mind.

As evidence of his divine power, Jesus eventually realized that he would be called upon to perform miracles of compassion and love. He did not do this for the gratification of curiosity seekers or disbelievers; but he performed these miracles for his own purposes.

I do not pretend to understand this wondrous part of Jesus' pastorate, and I do not believe it would matter even if I did. All I know is that herein lies another testament of his validity. There was never anything done by my Lord that would have been considered capricious or aberrant when it came to his performing a miracle. Instead, he did each thing as a measure of service for his fellow beings—that the afflicted might rise again as a completely whole person, that the maimed or beguiled might be healed—that they, and all who witnessed, would turn to him with gratitude and testimony.

"I cast out devils by the Spirit of God," he told me one evening when I inquired of him to understand these precious things. "I do among them the works which no other man can do."

This was true. No man had seen miracles so great as Jesus performed, for to that point, no man had the power or understanding that was his. It was a pure knowledge that gave him these powers—a perfect knowledge of things that worked together in the universe. No man would ever have so great a power unless he too were a God. Jesus said repeatedly that the glory of his Father was intelligence, and that we were all heirs to the father's knowledge if we would live honorably.

Merciful heavens, I considered. Could his message have been literal? Could we, in fact become gods by virtue of our accumulating all knowledge?

Always when speaking to us about his reasons for doing the things he did, Jesus gave credit and unrelenting acclaim unto his Father. He did nothing of himself. He would say this often. To God was given all honor and glory.

There was no selfishness in the heart of my Lord. None, whatsoever. I have scrutinized the various wonders performed for the welfare of the needy, and I am able to say, without restraint, that Jesus' heart was forever filled with compassion for us all. I thought . . . how could that be? How could any being here upon the earth be forever patient and unoffended by the perversions of men? How could Jesus turn a blind eye to the multitudes who sought to destroy him, or defile his spiritual acclaim?

Jesus' public ministry began between my home and his, in a

unique mountain village called Cana. It was the day of a wedding—a mutual friend's wedding—and a feast was prepared for all of us to enjoy. It was in the springtime, and the wild flowers, luminously colorful and fragrant, were everywhere.

As the warm, reassuring rays of the evening sun stretched a final time from behind the mountains to the west, a very energized Jesus stood near the synagogue. He had just descended from his home in Nazareth—the home that provided protection, learning, love, and finally opportunity for him to *know* of his unique identity.

"Greetings, my friends," he said warmly upon welcoming a couple that had entered the courtyard to the rear. "You have traveled from afar?"

"We have," replied one of the arrivals.

"Then you must have a place to rest and food to satisfy your hunger," Jesus offered with a familiar reassuring smile pursing his lips. "Come . . . join with us."

The affection of Jesus' eyes, the softness of his voice, and his straight forward civility startled the aging, weather-worn couple. They had traveled far—all the way from Capernaum, near the Galilean Sea, and they were weary from their journey.

Speaking first, the man replied. "You do us honor, my Lord," he said, then bowed reverently in front of Jesus. "God is good, and we have traveled safely through the valley, from our home in Capernaum. Our daughter just married a man called *Petra,* or Peter, and we have recently hosted their feast.

"We live near the synagogue, not far from the sea," the woman added, her dark veil still covering the better part of her face.

"The synagogue?"

"That is right, my Lord."

"And did you go there often?"

"We did, my Lord. We have wist that we could hear more

about thee!"

"I am but a carpenter from Nazareth . . ." the Savior said.

But the elderly couple knew otherwise.

"No sir," the older man exclaimed, "thou art *not* only a man. Thou art the promised Messiah, and we are exceedingly gratified to at last stand by thy side. Our lives we give to thee."

Jesus smiled. "Thou hast said well, my friend. Thy faith is strong. It shall serve thee well. Please enter here with us. We shall care for thee and thine."

"Thank you, my Lord."

Gesturing with an outstretched arm, he took the woman's cloak, placed it nearby, and invited them into the courtyard.

Jesus' mother confronted her gallant host-son. He was an inspiration. He was the embodiment of everything that was good. Nevertheless, in a frantic yet controlled voice, she, Mary, stepped up behind the Savior and cried out to him in despair. She was disturbed, and rightly so, for she had been asked to assist in the ongoing preparations of the feast. The wine—the very drink that would serve to nourish the invited guests—had been exhausted. More importantly, the remainder of the guests had arrived, and now were restless.

Sensing his mother's plight, Jesus raised a gentle hand as if to subdue her concerns. Speaking just loud enough for the couple from Capernaum to hear, he said, "All is well, mother. Please, allow me to enter with these weary travelers. Should we not see to their needs first?"

"Be it so, my son."

Lifting her skirt so as not to trip, Mary led the three into the courtyard where the guests were milling about. It was not far from the well from which the water, only moments before, had been drawn.

"If you would," Jesus then whispered, "take me to the water tureens. They have been filled, have they not?"

"Come with me, Jesus," his mother assured him. "Three firkins! The servants brought them from the well only moments ago. We have only water, I am aggrieved to say. We should have been better prepared."

"Worry not," Jesus consoled. His directive was not spoken with sharpness, nor with arrogance. Instead, it was phrased as a reassurance; and from many similar, though private such experiences in the past, his mother knew why.

Walking briskly behind Mary, Jesus turned toward the wooden table that offered the grape nectar. The empty wine containers. Wasting no time, but speaking at a volume that allowed the now hushed guests to hear, Jesus looked at the water in six water pots, and spoke.

"In the name of Israel's God, and by the power vested in the Son of God—let this water be turned to wine."

In that instant, the water drawn by the servants of the house, was indeed changed. It was water no longer, but a sweet variant of wine. Pausing only briefly, he added, "It is now so. Let us drink and honor the hosts who have brought us here this night."

When I learned of this first publically displayed miracle, I wondered why it was necessary, for truly it did not *heal* anyone. But in my heart I discovered, as I have so often since, that even at that early hour, Jesus showed a measure of compassion and service for those around him. This was no ordinary gathering of friends for fun or merriment. It was something quite sacred to the Lord, the personal nature of which has been lost in the sands of time. It was the gathering of a chosen two whose lives were about to be intertwined for all time. It was a couple in love. It was a bonding of two, whose hearts were one, and who had chosen to marry.

They had been friends of my Master, and earlier in the week had requested my Lord to attend. In so doing, Jesus clearly showed his approval of the marriage covenant. The ceremony brought tears to my eyes, for the words spoken were as consoling as the compassionate embrace of a mother's love. At the feast, Jesus admonished the couple to give themselves unselfishly and completely to one another, and to forever practice this custom. That by so doing, they would never fall away from their initial romantic appeal to one another. He admonished that if they abided by this law, they would never be persuaded to break the covenants of marriage.

I liked that.

On another occasion, when Jesus had returned to Galilee from Judea, a nobleman who had undoubtedly heard of his ability to heal the sick, came unto him—again from nearby Capernaum. He informed my Lord that he had a son who was ill with fever, and asked if Jesus would heal the child.

Jesus looked among the crowd that had gathered, and inquired as to whether they were desirous of witnessing the wonders of heaven. They chorused affirmatively.

The nobleman persuaded the Master to come with him and perform the sought-for miracle. But Jesus did not go with him. Instead, he looked directly into the eyes of the nobleman and inquired of him whether or not he believed.

"Yes, my Lord," the nobleman stated emphatically, "I do believe!"

Immediately, and without hesitation, the Savior said, "Return to thy home, for thy son will fare thee well. This day will he arise from his bed of sickness."

Upon hearing Jesus' words, the man did, in fact, hasten northward down the hill toward Capernaum. He did so with confidence, for he truly did believe that what Jesus had said would be done. Indeed, there was no misunderstanding, no misconception. Jesus had said that the man's son would be healed, and the Master's reputation had already reached far beyond the borders of our country. The man knew in his heart that it would be even as Jesus had commanded it to be. His son would be healed.

While journeying to Capernaum, the nobleman was met by his servants who had sought him by the roadside. They had been at the bedside of the afflicted child at the precise moment when Jesus had said that the boy would live, and had marveled at the sudden and unexpected healing that had taken place. For in that same hour, the boy's fever had left him, and he recovered completely.

Leprosy has been a common affliction of my people for as long as I can remember. It is a dreadful affliction that shows no mercy toward those scourged by it. Many have lived in fear of this awful plague, and have wondered if we would be the next victims of its desultory assault.

I have seen many wither away to their eventual deaths because of this bitter shadow of darkness, and have seen others cry out to the heavens for relief. No mortal should suffer this abomination, and no man or woman should have to die from its relentless grip. Nevertheless, many *do* die. All afflicted are consumed by its horrid clasp, for there is no panacea.

One day, while in Galilee, I was walking a little ways back from my Lord, when to my surprise a large crowd pressed in upon him. One among them was a leper. He was far gone, the poor man, and even *I* could see that his time was drawing nigh.

Mustering up what had to have been a tremendous amount of courage, the leper cried out to Jesus. "Please . . ." he wailed, "thou canst make me clean!"

Upon hearing this faith-inspired declaration, my Lord looked compassionately at the man while throngs of onlookers watched in wonder.

Inquiring of the leper, Jesus asked, "Believest thou this thing which thou asketh of me?"

"Certainly, Lord," the man exclaimed, tears falling freely

down his contorted cheeks. "I *do* believe!"

Knowing the defiled man's faith, Jesus healed him right there in the street.

Slowly, the stricken man lifted first his hands and fingers before his face. Then he beheld the rest of his crippled body. Before our eyes, all of his fingers returned, as if by magic, to their former state of wholeness. His entire body received the same blessing. Upon seeing himself cured, and while tears fell unabashed down his cheeks, the man cried out, "My Lord! My Lord! Oh, thank you, my Lord!" The man then turned and walked away from us all, never again to be so afflicted.

Jesus looked upon the man with compassion. He had instructed the leper to go his way and to tell no one of his healing, save it were a priest.

A priest? I asked myself.

At first I wondered why Jesus would impose such a restraint upon one who was so thankful. *Why not tell all the world the great news?* I pondered, *that others might come to Jesus and likewise be healed?* I soon learned that my Master wanted to be known for many *other* reasons, besides his ability to perform miracles; and that every time he did perform a miracle, he could no longer enter into that particular village, for he feared the safety of the multitudes that would push their way to see him.

For this reason, Jesus would occasionally withdraw into a solitary place of refuge and therein draw upon the powers of heaven. So often, throughout his ministry, I listened to this frequent injunction: "Tell no man what I have done for thee..."

Yet on nearly every occasion, the individuals receiving this blessing could not constrain themselves. They were overly elated by the miracles to which they had become a recipient, and with testimonies born anew wished to shout their healings from the rooftops.

Jesus, I think, knew that they would go straight away and tell all. Thus, he withdrew as often as his heart would tell him to do so, and would remain hidden until the chaos and disorder was dispelled. Nevertheless, there were times when he would instruct the recipient of a blessing to tell what had happened—and in so doing would remain in the area while others came unto him.

There were countless miracles performed by my Lord while I tarried with him, and at this time I will reflect on one or two more that played a role in my spiritual growth.

Most of my adult life was spent in the shadows of my Lord and Savior, for I knew and loved him as fervently as anyone I have known. I was drawn to him like the child is drawn to its father, and I feasted daily upon the personal instructions he proffered. His words and miracles showed me that he was surely who he claimed to be—the mortal Messiah!

Although so many of Jesus' miracles were performed on sinners and sufferers alike, there were circumstances that showed the whole world that he was the long-awaited Jehovah! I remember one such miracle—

The day had been long, and the night proved to be no less stressful for Jesus and his disciples. As their small fishing vessel pushed away from the shores of the Galilean Sea, near Capernaum, the men raised the sails to capture the winds, that they might press the vessel to sail easterly toward Gergesa. A storm of considerable magnitude suddenly arose out upon the waters. Such was the nature of the windy currents out upon the sea. It could be ever so calm; but then within a short breadth of time, the winds would abruptly change the tempest. During those unexpected moments, no vessel would be safe upon the waters. Such was the case on this night.

My dear friend, Simon Peter, chief among the apostles, was with Jesus during this frightening experience. He later shared the event with me—

"Mary," he said in reverent wonder, "may you remember that last night Jesus went out across the Sea of Galilee with our quorum members."

"I do," I submitted, remembering the bread I had baked for their journey.

"We set sail for Gergesa in the early evening, Mary. We thought that we would sail quickly for the winds did favor us, and our sails were filled to capacity with the strong breezes coming out of the west."

Continuing, he described the extraordinary scene with vivid detail. "When we had been underway for about a quarter of the night, a terrific wind arose and we were besieged by a great tempest. I thought that we would perish, for the sea did respond with a fury and a wrath, the likes of which I have never before seen. I thought that the devil himself had come to take us to the very gates of Hell, for so great was this storm."

"The gates of Hell?" I asked anxiously, knowing how dreadful the moment must have been for them.

"Mary," he continued, his hands quivering as he spoke, "as the waters continued to pound in around us and fill our vessel with heavy ballast, I went in unto Jesus, who had slept through the worst of it, and cried out to him for help. He awakened calmly and did not seem troubled by the events that were bearing in upon us. Though the ship tossed to and fro like a leaf driven by the wind, Jesus walked to the forward deck and simply stared into the sea.

"He stood there and stared, Mary.

"For a passage of time, he did nothing. Then," Peter added, his voice becoming increasingly excited, "just as we believed that we were doomed to suffer a horrible death, the Master stretched forth his hand and cried out to the very elements, themselves, as if they had a mind all their own! He said just three words, Mary! **'Peace, be still!'"**

"What happened next, Peter?"

"After our Lord did this thing, the waters immediately stopped tossing, the winds ceased to blow, and there went out across the waters a calm that was unlike anything I have ever witnessed. We were all confounded, and for our obvious lack of faith, the Lord rebuked us, then quieted us. I know that the Lord is a miracle worker, Mary, but I ask thee . . . what manner of man is he that even the winds and the seas listen and respond to his commands? You are his closest friend, and I thought you would want to know about this newest miracle. He is not of this world, Mary! I believe he is who he has said he is. He is the promised Messiah! It is he who has been prophesied of! He is a God!"

I thanked Peter genuinely, then excused myself.

Peter's bold temperament never ceased to surprise me, and I had to have time to assimilate his telling, though I already knew his words to be true.

Of this experience, I know little more than what Peter related to me, for my Lord never once spoke of it. I have since talked with several of the other disciples who were there, and each told me a similar tale. I have pondered such a miracle, and have reasoned that perhaps Peter was accurate in his bewildering assessment of the Lord when he asked, "What manner of man is this?" It is a thought that, without understanding, makes reason stare! He *is* the Lord of Hosts, and has the power to not only create the winds and the waters, but to subdue them, as well. It is a thought that still lingers through the recesses of my memories.

Indeed, what manner of man is this?

The Cleansing of the Temple

VIII

I return now to the beginning of my Lord's ministry, and share an experience that has recently been assuming an ever-increasing prominence in my mind.

Shortly after the marriage festivities in Cana, Jesus, together with his disciples, gathered together. They then walked north, to the home of Peter's mother-in-law, in Capernaum. Jesus had a vision that he described to his mother, Mary, on that occasion, and she shared it with me. His words led me to understand that his powers were even more extensive than I had first imagined.

Jesus, in his singular manner, was a prophet, seer, and revelator, for his eyes beheld many things that could not have been seen by any other man. As a God, he certainly would have had all of these wonderful powers manifest themselves; but on certain occasions his acts bore witness to his being a most powerful seer.

He knew all things.

Capernaum, a small village not far from Magdala, is situated near the northerly end of the Sea of Galilee. Prior to my Lord's ministry, the disbelief of the Jews therein became a source of great lamentation for him. After all, Jesus considered Capernaum to be his second home. In fact, he had found the brothers, Peter and Andrew, there, and also Matthew the tax collector. They thus became three of his chosen twelve.

As he tarried in Capernaum with these friends and followers, he made a prediction that exposed a deep sorrow in his heart. His mother, Mary, was with him at that moment, and she informed me that he came to a place overlooking the city, itself, and for a time watched the inhabitants therein. She told me that as Jesus looked on, tears welled up in his eyes and he wept.

"Why weepest thou, my son?" she consoled. But he said nothing to her. She had been many places with Jesus during his ministry, and had long since allowed him, without intervening, to go hither and thither as he felt impressed. Nevertheless, whenever she saw his sorrow or despair, she rallied, as any mother would, to comfort and protect him.

On this day however, she could neither provide comfort or persuade him to confide in her. For his eyes, she told me, had beheld a great judgment that was to come upon the people he loved and cared for in that village. After all, since beginning his public ministry, he called Capernaum his home. She told me that he saw the wickedness of the inhabitants of that fishing village, and witnessed their eventual destruction.

Jesus had hoped to tarry among the villagers and teach them the principles of the gospel, but said that they would not have him. Instead, he said that they would cast him out and possibly bring harm upon him and his followers if he even attempted to impart his doctrines. For this reason, Jesus turned his back on the city and left. This was during the time of the annual Passover, in Jerusalem, and in compliance with the Jewish law, he journeyed southward to that city. There was a great multitude in attendance at the Passover celebration, and an unusually gluttonous array of vendors gathered around the temple.

When Jesus arrived at what I now know to be his *holy house,* he stood before the open gates and marveled at the system of sale and barter that prevailed within the walls of the sacred edifice. He watched intently as greedy vendors capitalizing on the many stringent rules and regulations, convinced the faithful to buy and trade their offerings for the temple coin that was the only acceptable ransom offering allowed.

In the outer courts, hundreds of stalls filled with oxen and sheep, and cages with doves and pigeons gave testament to the fact that trade was charged for in complete measure. All males in Israel were required to pay the yearly ransom of half a shekel, irrespective of their impoverished condition. Since many did not have the money, traders posted in the temple courts rallied feverishly for a share of the incoming business. Moreover, the strict rules of the rabbis required that the payment be made in temple coin only—that no other heathen monies would be accepted.

The result of this strict imposition was that the moneychangers, themselves, developed a thriving trade on the holy grounds. This practice changed the spirit of the colossal Temple of Herod into a devilishly greedy marketplace with no spiritual serenity, whatsoever. During my Lord's lifetime, the holy temple priests performed only Aaronic priesthood ordinances there. This is why Jesus took Peter, James and John unto the Mount of Transfiguration—so that they could receive the higher priesthood keys in a place sanctified for that purpose. These keys—the very heart of the temple rituals—would *seal* families together for the eternities, a priesthood ordinance that up until this point could have only been performed by my Lord personally.

Jesus later told me that on that day of *transfiguration* the mountain *was* his temple. It was sacred and sanctified by God, himself. Still, performing the lesser priesthood ordinances inside Herod's temple required an acknowledged reverence for the Lord's spirit to dwell there.

Jesus could not tolerate the blasphemic vista before him, and quickly set about the task of improvising a strong whip of small cords. He moved in upon the vendors with a deftness, and boldly thundered a rebuke that was swift and sure. He liberated the animals caged round about, and overturned the tables of the moneychangers with a wrath that was exceedingly great.

My Lord was justly furious! Yet with tender regard for the safety of the birds, he refrained from assaulting their cages. Instead, he turned his anger on their owners and said: "Take these things hence!" To the greedy moneychangers he shouted yet another command that stung them to the core: "Make not my Father's house an house of merchandise!"

The scene was tumultuous and chaotic. Everywhere people were dashing about and trying, as best they could, to steer clear of the sting from Jesus' whip. Some of the moneychangers scrambled to recover what they still considered to be their rightful earnings. Yet the more they did this thing, the more angry Jesus became.

By and by, the multitude scattered. A great sense of dread began to sweep over the people, and they dared not intervene. Because of this assault, the devil began to take hold of the hearts of the indignant and angry onlookers. The same vendors who had lost their unholy earnings were wrath with my Lord and attempted to besiege his authority.

They were the foolish ones, for as they did these things, believing that they could intimidate Jesus, he rebuked them with a fierceness that did cause them to cower before him. Nevertheless, showing unrestrained benevolence for even those whose temperaments were not always honorable, Jesus showed forth an increase of love for all whom he had rebuked, then taught them the truths that were holy and right before God.

However, not all hearts were subdued. From that hour on, there were those who began to plot secretly against Jesus and sought to destroy him. These were the ambassadors of Lucifer.

Nevertheless, they did nothing at the moment, for they were afraid. Instead, they stood back in the shadows and watched and waited, silently conspiring against him until their hearts and minds were consumed with an anger and lust for vengeance.

After the temple had been cleansed, a group of adulterous priests and officials, whose charge it should have been to keep the temple sacred in the first place, approached Jesus with a measure of trepidation. They questioned whether he really had the jurisdiction to have done such a thing. In short, they wanted to know how he could claim such authority.

"What sign shewest thou unto us, seeing that thou doest these things?" they probed contemptuously.

Jesus, showing restraint for the obvious indignation, looked into their eyes and measured their inquisition. He understood the wickedness that was in their hearts and the future danger they imposed upon him. Nevertheless, with scant respect for their demand, he deftly replied, "Destroy this temple and in three days I will raise it up again."

Unwilling to acknowledge the Savior's authority, the angry priests took courage at what they perceived to be a blasphemous statement, and attempted to turn the crowds against him.

"Who art thou to come hither?" they cried aloud, invoking the anger of the moneychangers and those still gathered round about. "We are the children of the covenant . . . worshipers of the true and living God! *We* are the chosen over all the heathen and pagan peoples."

Jesus listened and held his tongue, for he was amazed at the pompous arrogance and self centered irreverence manifest in the proud leaders.

"Forty and six years was this temple in the building," they continued, "and wilt thou tear it down in three days?"

Jesus stood again and looked deeply into their eyes. He was angry, but said no more. For he had determined much earlier to never cast his pearls before swine. Moreover, he knew that they did not understand his prophetic utterance, for their ears were closed by their own wickedness. He had said what needed saying. He had done what needed doing. And with an unusually calm spirit about him, he promptly walked away from the scene, unmolested by anyone. Nonetheless, he knew that his words, chosen carefully on that day, would be used against him during some future event, and this troubled him deeply.

The evil priests would never forget; nor would they forgive. Jesus knew this, although he did not agonize or despair over the awareness. What had to be was already set in the heavens. It did not matter that the spirits of the damned conspired against him. For in his future, there were matters far more perilous than this.

It was almost three years later that my Lord stood before the governor of the land as an undefended prisoner. At that moment, the darkest perjury spoken against him came from a witness at the temple yard who said: "We heard him say that he would destroy the Temple of Herod, and in three days build it up again!"

Then, while the Lord hung in dismal suffering—for they eventually crucified him in a most devilish manner—the scoffers who passed by the cross shook their heads and taunted the dying Christ with: "Ah, thou that destroyest the temple and buildest it in three days; save thyself and come down from the cross."

These evil witnesses had no concept of the testimony of my Lord, for if they had, they would have concluded that he spake not of the temple of Herod, but of his own body of flesh and bone. He had been referring to the temple that was the temporary home of his immortal spirit. Even the disciples did not completely understand this message . . . that is, not until he was resurrected from the dead. For only then did they remember, and only then did they understand.

For now, my hand grows weary. I shall stop writing for a while. Then, after receiving nourishment and a good night's rest, I will continue. My words yearn to be spoken.

The Hospital in Tel Aviv, Israel

November 9, 1995

IX

By the time Melissa and I arrived at the hospital in Tel Aviv, we were prompted to stop just short of the recovery room. Inside, we could hear the weeping of several people, and we assumed them to be the Cohens.

"Shhhh," I whispered to Melissa. "Do you hear that?"

Immediately she understood what was happening, and shook her head in affirmation. Neither of us wanted to interrupt the family's exchange. Subsequently, we backed away from the door and remained outside the room.

We had not heard from the vexed rabbi, and now we knew why. Something had happened, had *changed*, and sensing this, we had once again borrowed a university van and had beelined it to Tel Aviv.

At that moment, a nurse came to the door and opened it just enough for us to peer inside. Sarah had the boy by the hand, and was caressing his fingers while she spoke to him in a most tender and tear-filled manner. The rabbi was standing quietly to the side, his arms enveloping their daughter, Rebecca.

"Dear Joseph, my precious son," Sarah cried. "1 know that I was not always the most patient mother for you. Perhaps it is because I always hoped that through a strict direction, your father and I could persuade you to listen to the prompting of the great one of Israel. We have only wanted you to grow in righteousness. We tried so hard, Joseph."

Melissa and I glanced at each other. Without speaking, we sensed that we had arrived too late. The way Sarah was speaking, we suddenly realized that Joseph Cohen was dead.

"My dear son," his mother continued, unaware of our presence in the doorway as she wept her dialogue, "I want you to understand the great thing your father and I have learned. You see, we are no longer persuaded to believe in the traditions of our fathers. Instead, as our American friends have continued their work on the Magdalene parchments, we have discovered how terribly fallacious our traditions have been.

"Oh, Joseph . . . dear, dear son. Do you know how brave you were to shelter Rebecca? Do you know that Jesus is watching over you right now, even as we speak? He knows what you did. He knows that because of your willingness to give your own life for the life of your sister, you are a special spirit. How great shall be your reward!

"Somehow, Joseph, I know that you can hear my voice. I feel that you are here with us even though we cannot speak with one another. The Savior of the world, Jesus Christ, is with you always, for I sense a most powerful spirit from you."

Sarah suddenly dropped her head down onto the chest of her son, Joseph, and began to cry. Her grief was full and inconsolable. She knew that, like Mrs. Rabin, she had lost her loved one to an assassin's bullet.

Although we did not feel it right to intervene, Melissa and I craned our necks to take a peek into the hospital room. At that moment, Rabbi Cohen looked up and saw us. Leaving his daughter's side, he staggered toward us, his arms outstretched.

"Oh, Jason!" he blurted, his chest heaving as he drew in great gulps of air. "He is gone! Our Joseph is dead!"

Professor Cohen was a man of uncommon faith, yet at this unfortunate hour he was also a father wracked with a pain so deep that he could not contain himself. Collapsing in my arms, it was all I could do to hold him up. He slumped over and sobbed so deeply that I could only join in. Melissa, sensing her own role of comfort, dashed past us and threw her arms around Sarah and Rebecca. It was a scene never to be forgotten, and one that is etched in the most pain-filled recesses of my heart.

Finally, when the anguishing professor regained his composure, he slumped into the nearest chair. "My Joseph is gone," he moaned. "All our prayers . . . they made no difference. The power of Jesus Christ . . . where is it? Perhaps it is hidden beneath a rock in Gethsemane."

The next hour of my life was *deja vu*. I was reliving the hell of losing Kirsten all over again. This time, however, I was not simply dealing with my own untimely loss. I was having to cope with the bitter supposed betrayal of a new Christian man in the unjust loss of his son. I felt utterly helpless, and longed to escape into my own private closet. But there was no closet. There was only a hospital room, a deceased loved one, and a grieving family.

Melissa felt at a loss, as well. After quietly visiting with her in the hallway while the Cohen family spent a final few minutes with Joseph, I made arrangements to drive the rabbi and his family back to Jerusalem, with Melissa following close behind in the university van. The arrangements were her idea, actually, and I appreciated her astute thinking at this precarious hour.

A cloud of sadness hovered over us as arrangements were made for young Joseph's remains to be taken to Jerusalem. With this ordeal over, the hour-long trip back to the Cohen's home transpired without incident. After spending the evening with them, as they planned the funeral, Melissa and I drove back to the university in somber silence. The entire afternoon had been an unexpected nightmare, and we could both sense that the pain—and the manner in which we dealt with Rabbi Cohen's anger—was only beginning. For each of us, in our own way, the hour could not have been more bleak.

To say that the next week was traumatic would be an understatement. The funeral, the paralyzed university, the continued state of shock for the state of Israel and for the Middle East. The entire region reeled in unison with the Cohen family, as Rabin's and Joseph's deaths were almost impossible to deal with.

As for the rabbi, himself, there was a brewing bitterness that seemed to accelerate with each passing day. The funeral brought no resolution. Prayers ceased. Darkness closed in.

While Melissa and I spent as much time with the Cohen family as we could, the professor finally asked us to proceed with the translation of the scrolls, while allowing him and his family to mourn in solitude. It was not a solution that Melissa and I would have chosen, but we had no choice but to comply with Rabbi Cohen's request.

And so, with unresolved knots in the pits of our stomachs, the two of us spent the Sabbath with each other, and attending church services, then settled into the routine of translating the following morning. We both agreed that it would be therapeutic for us to resume our work with the ancient Mary's record, and we welcomed the respite from the lonely anguish that we felt for the Cohen family. The only thing we knew—or that we *thought* we knew—was the peace young Joseph must be experiencing as he became oriented in the world of spirits. "Who knows," I whispered to Melissa, as we began translating, "maybe he'll even get to meet Kirsten. They could become the very best of friends..."

Unbeknown to me, Melissa wasn't listening. Although she nodded in acknowledgment of my comment, her thoughts were two thousand years away. She was considering a statement the ancient Mary had made about reliving the bitterness of the apparent mistakes of her youth. It would be days before Melissa would share her discovery with me.

For now, however, she simply turned on the computer and readied herself to transcribe the final portion of Mary's second set of scrolls.

LAZARUS
North of Magdala on the Slopes to Capernaum
68 A.D.

X

Stars!

Millions and millions of stars, forever reaching into the vast expanse of the heavens. Worlds without ends, kingdoms spanning the endless firmament, yet each one accounted for and individually numbered by the Father—

I marvel at this.

Who can look upon the stars in this majestic vastness of the Lord's domain and believe that anything other than a Supreme being with all knowledge and wisdom created the same? Surely it was a God of love for his children who did this great thing. Could it be anything more than this? I think not.

These days I can hardly refrain from gazing into the heavens.

The stars! Look upon them, and see the throne of God!

I recall to mind a spiritually invigorating moment I shared with Jesus, decades ago, here upon the slopes of the hills overlooking the village of Capernaum. Together we have seen the brilliance of the stars many times from this very place. Sitting on a tuft of grass, and remembering what many have called *The Sermon on the Mount* as my Lord spake it here so many years ago, brings a measure of languor to my soul, for I miss him more and more with each passing day. His message was replete with joy and hope.

On this day, I am aggrieved to say, I do not feel either. Instead, I am experiencing a sense of loneliness that is oppressive. Oh, how I miss my Lord. How I miss his gentle touch, his caring words, his knowing eyes—

Though filled with anguish, I find myself reflecting upon perhaps one of the crowning moments of my Lord's miracle ministry. It happened just a week before his death during a time that I was visiting with my friends, Lazarus, Mary, and Martha. It was an unusually warm night. For the third time in a short while—under the loving and watchful eyes of God—my Lord had called upon the holiest of powers. With great humility and confidence abounding, he had shown to all the world that, even in death, God's powers were available to all of the children of men through faith.

He had been able to provide a glimpse into his own future. He had been allowed to teach each of us, and those who would learn thereafter, that life itself was eternal! He had been able to show, through the miracle he performed, that Father's children would begin to understand the true significance of his impending death and resurrection.

Death and resurrection!

To each of us, there must be a testimony given in order to understand this eminent gift. It is not for me to say any more than I already have on the matter. But I remain humbled, even overwhelmed by his love for me; that he has assured me of his gift to us all!

I say again, my Lord promised that he would not remain in the grave, but that he would be resurrected. And what meaneth the holy resurrection? It is the completion of that gift that Jesus has bestowed upon all of us. It is the rejoining of the body and the spirit of man. Such bringing together creates the *soul* of man. Think of it— Each of us will die! Each will be given back to the earth, and yet, all will live! How is this possible? How is it conceivable for the body to reunite itself with the spirit after death? It is a matter of power. That is all I know . . . and of course it is a matter of promise. For Jesus told me that all of the children of men shall be resurrected, that the experience was a universal gift unto all men, including sinners.

Nevertheless, there is the difference of this resurrection and the gift that will be given to the righteous, the gift of eternal life or eternal salvation. Not all will be saved in the kingdom of the Father! To be a part of this great promise from the heavens, Jesus told me that I must live the commandments. I must serve my brothers and my sisters of the earth. He even counseled me to tell others to live like he lived, to do as he would do, and in all ways to give thanks to the Father.

Oh, blessed Jesus. He seemed to want nothing of himself, but for his Father he wished all things virtuous.

Jesus marveled at his Father's power that, in truth, had become *his* power. In reverent adoration, Jesus thanked God for having allowed his hands to be the instruments for so magnificent an event. In the eyes of those present, he demonstrated God's power over death and the timelessly misunderstood concept of the grave. Furthermore, he said that he would provide this most impressive blessing to all who believed in him.

It had been an emotion-packed two days for the Worker of Miracles, yet they were two of the most gratifying days of his mortal ministry. For, in response to the request of our friends of Bethany, Mary and Martha, Jesus had traveled quickly to where we were gathered in mourning.

Lazarus, Jesus' lifelong friend and companion, had suffered a demon fire of the mind. He had grown weak from the fever and had not survived. He had expired. He had been buried two days earlier in the hillside dungeon tomb, in Bethany. Each of Lazarus' friends had hoped that Jesus would have come sooner, that perhaps he might have been able to save Lazarus—that he might have cast out the fever just as he had done for others during his ministry.

But when Jesus arrived at the tomb, he found Lazarus dead, wrapped in burial cloth and laid to rest deep inside the dark and lonely sepulcher.

"Lazarus," he whispered quietly, while crawling down to the side of our friend. Somehow he was speaking to Lazarus' departed spirit. "How I have missed thee. How I have longed for the days of our youth, when we played as children, when we ate bread, and when we read the sacred writings together!

"Thy sisters sent for me four days ago," he continued, glancing up in our direction, "and told me of thy illness. I knew that thou hadst died, even as they told me it was so. But I could not come unto thee, Lazarus, despite my longing to do so. I was two days constrained before beginning the journey, for the miracle had to be complete.

"Forgive me, my friend, but know that it was for the purposes of the Father that I have been delayed; for through His matchless powers manifest here today, many will experience a mighty change of heart, and will begin to comprehend the glory of the Father."

As Jesus related to us later that night, never in all his mortal life had he called upon the powers of God for so great a miracle. Life over death after the body had begun to decay! The concept, and now the reality of the event, was staggering. Jesus then recalled two similar miracles he had performed earlier in his ministry. He had raised Jairus's daughter, as well as the son of the widow of Nain, from the dead. They had only recently died, of course, and many had not believed. But now, with Lazarus, he must leave no doubt. For, by waiting four days, Lazarus' body was decomposing. This was significant, since our Jewish tradition claimed that a person's spirit departed their presence by that time. And so he had shown, once and for all, his power over life.

Lazarus' sister, Martha, was the one who had retrieved my Lord. Upon locating him near the River Jordan, she had earnestly pleaded, "If thou hadst been here, Master, Lazarus would not have died!"

Before Jesus had been able to respond, the simplicity and grandeur of Martha's heartfelt faith had been manifest. As he later related, this was a sweet and refreshing moment for him; for here, unlike so many of the others with whom he'd conversed, was a common man with a heart of pure gold. In a tender, personal way, Jesus had been allowed to reply.

"Thy brother shall rise again," he had said simply. Although the message had been intended to instill hope into Martha's heart unlike anything she had ever before experienced, Jesus noted that even then she had not fully understood.

"I know that he shall rise again," she had replied tenderly, "in the resurrection at the last day. Even so—"

"I am the resurrection and the life," Jesus had affirmed joyously. "He that believeth in me, though he were dead, yet shall he live!"

It was only a short while after meeting with Martha that Jesus came, at last, to where Mary was grieving the loss of their brother. I was with her, in the mourner's chamber; but even so, she was inconsolate. She too had been an affectionate disciple of the mortal Messiah, and had also pleaded with him to do what he could.

"Where have ye laid him?" Jesus inquired of Mary, while I sat silently in a remote corner of the chamber. Pleading for his intercession—or at least his understanding—they pointed toward the opening that descended into Lazarus' tomb. At the sight of the grave, Jesus felt the powerful strains of love well up inside him. Almost immediately, he too wept openly. Lazarus had been a lifelong friend. But now, as we all could see, he was dead—

Death! For most of his Father's children, Jesus knew that the event was sadly misunderstood. He knew that it was mistakenly compared to so many of the human experiences, when the end of a certain advent brought with it a disturbing sense of finality. Nevertheless, death was *not* final. Jesus knew this, and in his heart he sensed that most of us, if not all, knew it, too.

"Take ye away the stone," he commanded the two men who stood nearby. Martha, however, was immediately apprehensive.

"Wait!" she countered nervously. "Lord, by this time he stinketh, for he hath been dead four days."

In Martha's heart, she did believe that it was too late. Lazarus *was* dead—four days dead. Already his corpse was decaying in its tomb. How could anyone, including Jesus, repair the body, or in fact restore it to life?

But Jesus had sensed her concern, and had made every effort to show compassion for her. He loved her as he loved Mary and their departed brother. He would not cause her further heartache.

"Said I not unto thee that if thou wouldst believe, thou shouldst see the glory of God?" These were his words of affectionate warmth to his troubled friend, while using the hem of his garment to tenderly wipe the tears from her cheeks.

Jesus had known that the moment was ripe, for all around us were friends of the family—Jews from the city—curious onlookers whose hopes were kindled, but whose hearts were understandably cautious concerning this Miracle Worker from far away Nazareth.

When the stone had been removed from Lazarus' grave, something besides Lazarus' mummified remains had caught Jesus' eye. It had not distracted him from the magnificent task at hand, but had sparked a subtle and warm memory.

For only a moment, Jesus had looked upon the wooden artifice with emotional affection, allowing the brief recollection of events long past to soothe his soul. For, well did he recognize the object, and recall the very hour when he had presented the gift to his friend, Lazarus. There, leaning up against the stone wall of Lazarus' tomb, was the solid oak walking stick Jesus had crafted with his own hands while working as the Carpenter's Son in Nazareth.

The staff! It reminded Jesus of his family, his home, and days long gone.

"Mary," he said humbly, "all these years and still Lazarus has not misplaced, discarded, or abandoned my gift—this wooden staff."

"No, my Lord. He has carried it since the earliest days of our youth . . . all the way to his four-day tomb."

At that moment, Lazarus' wrapped and anointed remains were lifted through the opening of the tomb. It was then placed gently on the floor of the mourning chamber for all present to see. For a moment, even *I* had my doubts.

Eyes watched. Hearts beat rapidly. Then, before we could situate ourselves comfortably for the once-of-a-lifetime miracle we all were praying to see, Jesus lifted his eyes heavenward, and spoke almost in a whisper. "Father, I thank thee that thou hast heard me. And I know that thou hearest me always; but because of the people who standest by, I said it, that they might believe that thou hast sent me."

When he had spoken to his Father in plain view of all present, Jesus looked around one last time. He wiped away another tear that had fallen from the eyes of the lovely Martha, then cried out with a penetrating voice that seemed to shake the very foundations of the earth—

"Lazarus!" He commanded, "Come forth!"

And Lazarus did come forth, opening first his eyes as the

cloth was removed. A sudden shivering response caused him to twitch and shake his head back and forth. Then, as if rising from the drunkenness of an early morning sleep, he sat upright and turned his head toward Jesus, caught up in the wonderment of being alive.

Their eyes made contact. It was an impossible thing, but nevertheless it happened! Lazarus stood to greet our Lord.

"Master . . ." was all he could say. But that was enough.

Smiling warmly, Jesus drew his arms around Lazarus. He then did something unexpected. He grasped the staff that had been leaning in the corner of the chamber, and handed it to Lazarus.

"Here, Lazarus. I believe this is yours."

Slowly comprehending my Lord's statement, Lazarus stabled himself with the cane. It was the same cane Jesus had made for him, and given to him, while on their first trip to Jerusalem's Feast of the Passover. That had been when he was but ten years of age, and Jesus twelve. But here it was, a token of his continued mortal breathings, and a symbol of his reliance upon my Lord as the True Staff of Life. Above all, it was an image of the Savior's love.

Jesus then supported Lazarus as they made their way slowly up the stairs and into the dirt-packed street above. The miracle had taken place, and now my Lord was filled with joy of a different nature.

Lazarus, one of Jesus' dearest friends, was alive!

Later in the afternoon, as Jesus seated himself near the top of a grassy knoll, he invited me to visit with him. There he was contemplating the relative quiet that, for the moment, was his. It was much needed solitude; for although he had been deeply gratified by the miraculous event of Lazarus' rebirth into mortality, he had fallen into a cloud of despair. Something that

I knew nothing about was tormenting him.

"What troubles thee, my Lord?"

He looked lovingly into my eyes and acknowledged my inquiry. But then he told me not to worry.

"But I love thee, Jesus. And if there is something that troubles thine heart this night, then I should like to comfort thee."

He then explained that he had been contemplating the wickedness of the world. He said that he understood the evil in certain men's hearts, and that there would be a season of darkness in his immediate future.

"What darkness, my Lord?"

"Be ye not troubled Mary, for I do what I must do for the salvation of the children of men."

I still did not understand. He told me how he had prepared himself for the ominous moments ahead—the mental and physical sacrifice that had been ordained for him since the beginning of time. He declared that he was not troubled, but humbled, even thankful to be of service to the Father.

"Mary," he rejoined quietly, "Lazarus is alive because of the matchless powers of the Almighty! While raising Lazarus from the dead has changed the hearts of many, still I fear that others at the grave site were not convinced. To the contrary, they consider me even a greater threat to their security than they did before I arrived."

Jesus, of course, was right. Word was even then spreading quickly to the Chief Priests and Pharisees. Although I was unaware of it, a council was convening that very moment, making plans to eliminate my Lord. For him, the pain was heart felt and consuming. No longer would familiar, friendly places be a safe haven for him. Instead, our homes would become dangerous locations, and become subjected to the callous and deadly whims of the Roman soldiers. In fact, from this moment forward, Jesus understood that he would have to walk cautiously, even among those he called "my own."

With these thoughts in mind, Jesus announced that he would leave Bethany. His plan was to depart the following morning, and travel up through the country near the city of Ephraim. There he would continue his work with his disciples. After all, it was the very act of teaching and giving to others that brought such contentment to his heart. There was no time to worry about what pains he would have to endure—not while there was still time to unite families, change hearts, heal the sick, and lift the weary.

"Lazarus!" my Lord suddenly exclaimed. "Lazarus, dear Lazarus, is *alive!* Mary, this is a time of rejoicing, an epochal moment of triumph!"

An affectionate smile spread across my Lord's face, as in his mind he relived the extraordinary event of the previous afternoon. How truly wonderful it had been to look upon the faces of those present. Such wonder and hope had been provided for so many.

"Oh, Jesus," Mary voiced timorously, "Thou art the Christ. My heart is filled with such hope as I have never before known. There is great joy in my heart, Master."

"Men are that they might have joy," he replied, staring off into space. "It is my Father's way."

By now, Martha and Mary, who dearly loved Lazarus, had led him back to their home. Though Lazarus was understandably weak and needing nourishment, he and his sisters were experiencing the ethereal joy of a family reunited.

That was what it was all about, really . . . homes and families! The children of men united together under the protective and loving care of their fathers and mothers. That was where the real joy of life's journey was founded—inside the home! I knew it then, and wish the entire world would know it now.

Families!

Jesus lay down atop the grassy hillside and again stared up at the stars. "Tonight, Mary," he whispered, "I will forget about the hostilities which lurk in the shadows of men's hearts. I will rest from my labors, and I will travel back to a more simple time—a day when life was less demanding and oh, so very joyous . . . .

Moments passed, while my Lord considered the mortal life that had been his. He knew that in many people's lives, he had been an example of great good; and if nothing else, he hoped they would remember him for the charitable soul that he was.

"Charity," he mouthed audibly. Without expecting a reply, he then closed his eyes and inwardly pled with his Heavenly Father to instill that single virtue into the hearts of his numerous brothers and sisters around the world. That was what it was all about, he was sure of it. Charity, the purest form of love would change them all.

Slowly, then, without seeming to remember that I was present, the tired and emotion-filled Savior of the world drifted over the edge of sleep. And as he did, he pictured in his mind a quaint shop at the edge of town, where in the corner, he had only moments before placed the finished staff—the walking stick he had fashioned for his friend, Lazarus of Bethany.

As I make an end to my writings this night, I feel wondrously close to the spirit of my departed Lord and Master. I feel the memories of our time together with a strong sense of personal emotion. My heart is filled with gratitude for the opportunity of chronicling the events of His life as I remember them.

I am once again like a little girl. I cry easily. I remember the simplest things with Jesus at my side, and think it all a dream. Still, I know that it was not a dream. I know that he lived here with us. I know that his spirit lingers still. I see him in my dreams, and he speaks to me while I write the words of this record.

Tears! My visage is bathed in tears! My reminiscence—my

mental transportation through time to the very hour of my Lord's greatest miracle—has been so real to have produced torrents of tears. But they are soothing to my soul, for I know that he lives!

Jesus of Nazareth, he to whom I last spoke at the Garden Tomb on the morning of his resurrection, is *not* ministering on a distant orb in the universe. He was here but moments ago, and his Holy Spirit bears record of it. He was here at my side, guiding me through details of his greatest miracle, so that others might know.

What could be better than this?

I am at peace, so for now I bid farewell. I will resume my writing on another day. It will be my final task to share the events of my Lord's final week in mortality. For now, however, I will savor the moment—the hour I was visited by my Lord.

Part Three

THE CONCEALMENT

Hebrew University Library Archives

November 23, 1995

I

Melissa looked over at me with an expression of love. She had finished transcribing the final words of Mary's remarkable account of the Lazarus miracle. I could tell that she had been moved to tears by the words of the ancient feminine scribe, and I felt gratified to have been sitting at her side as the scenes from Mary's scrolls came alive for us—especially since Mary shared such a personal impression of a visitation by Jesus, himself.

"Can you believe it?" Melissa exclaimed, her lower jaw agape with wonder.

"Yes," I responded, looking at Melissa who, at that moment, was conceptualizing all of the final translated hieroglyphic figures on the computer screen before her. We had already read every thing there was to read up to that point.

I again spoke. "From the dead? His friend, Lazarus? That confirms it then."

"Confirms what?" Melissa questioned.

"Jesus. It seems to me that if the Bible was even remotely accurate, then we have another witness to that fact right here in front of our very eyes! I mean, this could be big, Missy . . . really big! Are you hearing me?"

"Yes!" she echoed, her voice rising more and more to that infamous Melissa Jones-having-just-discovered-something-really-important pitch.

At that instant, the door to the library archives swung open.

Melissa and I spun around in our swivel-style desk chairs, and captured a most unusual picture. The intruder was the professor, himself, and though we would normally have been delighted to see him after his long absence since Joseph Cohen's funeral, there was something very different about the old man.

His face was sullen. His eyes were aflame with a redness that spoke of an anger that I could not decipher. Actually, it might have been something totally foreign to anger. I just didn't know—that is, not until the other two skeptical Jewish rabbis entered the library directly behind the professor. They were the same professors who had protested the scroll's translation the week before. They too seemed highly volatile, and definitely cantankerous. Indeed, the three of them looked as if they were going to explode!

"Pro . . . fffessor?" I managed.

The generally good-hearted rabbi, Eli Cohen, walked quickly to my side. Speaking firmly, and with perspiration dripping onto his beard, he began. "You have been translating a ruse, Jason, and we cannot tolerate this kind of pseudo-intellectual activity at Hebrew University. You and Melissa must discontinue your project at once. The final two sets of scrolls will be sealed in the condition you now leave them. Your dissertation explaining the first set of scrolls can be completed, as promised. Melissa can complete her dissertation, and your studies here will then come to a close."

"Excuse me, Professor," I countered, trying to understand what was happening. "I'm afraid I don't understand. What do you mean?"

"It means, Jason, that you have been bewitched by a woman. It means, after coming to an understanding with the administration at the university, that the work of a woman cannot validate so unrealistic a claim! There might have been a historical figure who could have been the finest scholastic rabbi of his day—a noble teacher and proven Pharisee named Jesus. He may very well have been inspired by the great Jehovah, or even by God. While it is a shame that he was crucified, he was *not* the promised Messiah."

"But, Rabbi—"

"Listen to me, Jason. You are a good student. Both of you are good students. But the work of Mary, from ancient Magdala, is the work of a woman. It is nothing more."

Stunned, Melissa interrupted, questioning. "Oh? And what exactly does that—"

"It means, Melissa," one of the other professors interjected, "that it cannot be substantiated work. The elders at the time of your Jesus were the only authorized record keepers of prophetic truths. It has always been that way, and until the holy Messiah comes, it will remain that way.

"We, the leaders of our faith, are the record bearers. We do not rely upon the words of our women to record our lives and our histories. It is the tradition of our elders, and it shall remain intact."

"Please, my friends," Rabbi Cohen pleaded, now softening as he stroked his moistening beard. "Ours is a special friendship, and it will remain so. You must trust the decisions that have been made. Please, come with us . . . ."

Aghast, I simply stared ahead. I could not believe what was happening, yet I knew that the person facing me was *not* Rabbi Cohen. It was his body, perhaps, and even his voice. But it was not his soul, that was certain! The strain of Joseph's death had finally taken its toll, and more than anything else, I ached for the result. Rabbi Cohen, and his family, were suffering at a depth that even I could not comprehend. The pain had to be unbearable.

The Magdalene scrolls, together with the files and computer disks already marked and catalogued, were left alone on the table in the center of the room. The door to the vault-like office was closed behind us as we walked out into the hallway. The lights were then turned out.

For now, the work on the scrolls was as complete as it would be.

While the computers we had been using were assumed to be turned off, it was not so. Their terminals had been idle, and had merely fallen into a 'sleep' mode. Moments after we left the library archives, a furtive figure emerged from behind the files in the back of the archive room.

Moments later, the person's olive complexioned fingers worked tentatively on the keyboard until the screen illuminated and a password was required for further access. The darkly dressed keyboard operator punched in the word: KIRSTEN.

"Bleeeeep!"

The computer's access code sputtered, then opened the document last utilized by Jason Ellis. The words: **The Carpenter's Son I & II** appeared. Below, an entire volume of translated text from the Magdalene scrolls, were written in perfect English. The first set of scrolls was duplicated on the first disk, and the second set of scrolls on the other.

A transfer of the two files was made to the A-Drive disc, the computer was turned off, and the dark-dressed intruder exited the room.

The Ultimate Support
November 24, 1995

II

Fours hours later Melissa and I were still reeling from what had taken place with Rabbi Cohen. Nibbling on felafels at the fast food stand on Lehi Street, we decided to change the subject. We were exhausted, and it was the only way we could cope—

"Missy," I began, after a full minute of silence, "tell me about Mary's comment."

"I'm not sure I follow, I—"

"You know, her statement about remembering the mistakes of her youth."

Measuring my eyes, Melissa could see that I was in earnest. Pausing briefly, she picked at her felafel, then began. "She made several comments, actually, including her memory of having evil spirits expelled from her. Whatever her problems, it is obvious that she remembered them."

"What are you saying, Melissa?"

"What I'm *trying* to say is that she had her ghosts, too. More importantly—"

Suddenly Melissa couldn't speak. Tears welled in her eyes,

and she swallowed hard. Not wanting to push her, I remained silent. When at last she gained control, she continued. "More importantly, Jason, she wrote with *hope.* She just didn't write about it, but her record was replete with it. Her heart was good, and it was at peace."

"So, what are you saying?"

"I'm saying that Mary had an assurance in the atonement. Christ was not just a father figure to her, but he was her personal Savior."

It was my turn to have blurry vision. Wiping the corners of my eyes, I waited for her to complete her statement. When at last she spoke, it was following a deep breath.

"I have spent hours on my knees, Jason, praying for what Mary *had.* Believe me when I say that it's here. Deep in my heart I have a burning that is unlike anything I have ever known. It's why I was so quiet today, during our final moments of translating."

"I am so happy for you, Missy. In spite of all that's happening with Rabbi Cohen and the ancient record, the most important thing is your happiness . . . your peace of mind."

"Thank you, Jason. What you have just said means more to me than all the ancient manuscripts in the world."

I was just taking Melissa's hand to help her to her feet when a white taxi came screeching around the corner. Pulling to a stop, neither of us could have been more surprised to see none other than Sarah Cohen climb out of the car. Glancing first toward the dorms across the street, she was just stepping off the curb when I called her name. "Mrs. Cohen, over here! We're over here!"

Recognizing us, she waved and almost ran to where we were sitting. Gasping, she placed a yellow padded envelope onto our table. "Eli sent me," she sighed. "This is for you."

To say that we were dumbfounded would be an understatement. Sarah Cohen was the *last* person we expected to see—especially alone on the streets of Jerusalem, after dark.

"I'm afraid I don't understand," I questioned.

"He is so ashamed. He knows that he betrayed your trust, but his peers put on so much pressure. Most of all, he knows that he lied. He betrayed our Lord, our Savior and King."

Until this moment, Melissa had remained silent. She could scarcely lace the information together. But now, having heard Sarah Cohen's admission, she blurted: "Another Peter! Professor Cohen renounced his testimony of Christ."

"Easy, Missy," I cautioned. "The rabbi is under unbelievable stress."

"Melissa is right." Sarah Cohen confirmed the analogy, then added, "He also betrayed the promise he made to his father, on his father's deathbed. With Joseph's passing, he no longer cares to live. It is as if his candle no longer burns."

Wanting very much to console the professor's wife, all I could manage was, "It will all work out. One day the scrolls will be published, and he will affirm their authenticity. He will also confess the Lord, and him crucified. Your husband is one of the greatest men I have known, Sarah, and none of that changed today."

"Oh, Jason, thank you!" Mrs. Cohen cried. "My Eli has lost all faith in himself, and he acts as though his life were over."

"I plan on coming over later this evening, Sarah. I have something to share with him—two things, actually. One is a gift, and the other is a loan. Would that be alright?"

"Uh . . . but of course. I can't guarantee that Eli will see you, but please come. In the meanwhile, know that I copied both sets of translated scrolls today, after you left the library. It was Eli's request, and now it is his gift to *you*. You are free to publish the second set of scrolls as you both wish . . . with how do you say it? . . . no strings attached."

"Thank you," we chorused.

The conversation abruptly ended, and almost as mysteriously as she had arrived, Sarah Cohen returned to the waiting taxi, and sped toward the Hyatt Regency turn-around. Seconds later, the car sped past Eidelsen dorms, blinked its lights in our direction, then wound its way down off of French Hill.

Melissa, quick to judgment, at once challenged the experience. "The rabbi is just salving his conscience. He's looking for a way out."

"He thought of it before he expelled us, Missy. Sarah was there to retrieve our efforts on disc. That doesn't sound like a man who is salving *anything*."

"Perhaps you're right. I'm just so astonished by this that I can't digest it."

"The game's not over, Missy. Professor Cohen is behaving irrationally, but only from our perspective. His only son has been killed, he is taking flack from the conservative faction on the faculty, and he just snapped. He'll be back, if only we don't desert him. He would do no less for us if the tables were turned."

Looking me squarely in the eyes, Melissa did not speak. Instead, she threw her arms around me and buried her face in my chest. "You are so good, Jason, so Christlike. Thank you for being so . . . *you.*"

An hour later, after speeding through the streets of Jerusalem in my own rented taxi, I motioned for the driver to pull over. "I'll be just a minute, sir. Here are more shekels than you'll make all night. Please wait for me."

Without waiting for a reply, and trusting in the decency of the driver, I climbed out of the car and bounded up the stairs to Rabbi Cohen's door. Knocking gingerly, I was not surprised when Sarah Cohen answered.

"Hello, Jason. Eli has gone to bed with a migraine. Please

understand. He will come around, it is my word."

Handing Sarah first an envelope, then the Lazarus staff, I forced my hands to my side, and then spoke. "The message inside the envelope is for all of you. Melissa and I wrote it together, and we did so with loving candor. As for the staff, that is just a loan; a symbol, actually. Your husband gave it to me months ago, but I am not comfortable having it in my dorm. Besides, it seems to have a life of its own—and always seems to be used with a purpose—so invite the good rabbi to keep it close to him. I'll pick it back up in a few weeks, before I leave for the states."

"Thank you, Jason," Sarah whispered, a tear of acknowledgment already working its way down her cheek. "I think I know what it is for, and I will pass your words along."

Clearing my throat, and bringing my own emotions under control, I concluded. "One more thing, Sarah. Tell your husband—a man I love as I do my own father—that he is one of the purest Christians I have ever known."

Yet another hour later, at the very moment when I was brushing my teeth in preparation for bed, on the other side of Jerusalem Rabbi Eli Cohen re-read the tear-stained letter for the fifth time. I was unaware of his actions, of course, but somehow I hoped that such was the case.

The letter was brief, but spoke from our hearts. It read:

Dear Rabbi Cohen,

It is getting late, so we will be brief. We just want to again express our sorrow in the passing of your Joseph. He is one of our true friends, and we look forward to one day renewing our love for him. Thank you for rearing such a remarkably gifted and righteous young man. He is busy now, we're sure—but perhaps every now and again he can take time off to see how you are doing.

It occurred to us this afternoon that just as Joseph gave his life for Rebecca, so also did Jesus give his life for mankind. What a remarkable parallel!

As for the Lazarus staff, please don't become too attached to it. It is no longer yours, as you know, but must be protected until it returns to the states. If you would like to lean on it, then please do. Only don't feel as though you must gather support from it in public. The timing's not right. Just use it in your home, especially just prior to family prayer. That way it'll never get broken.

All our love and loyalty,

Melissa and Jason
Your devoted students

P.S. Perhaps you can even share the staff with Sarah and Rebecca. We think they would like that.

As Rabbi Cohen finished his fifth reading of the letter, he slowly folded it and placed it back inside the envelope. Glancing at the ancient, gnarled staff, he managed to lift it into his lap. Then, without so much as a blink, his eyes riveted on the time-honored 'Lazarus' inscription written by the youthful Jesus two thousand years before. For just an instant his eyes seemed to moisten. He took a short breath, then a long one, and almost immediately fell into a deep sleep. For the first time in weeks his muscles relaxed, the lines in his face softened, and the rhythm of his breathing spoke volumes.

Nor did Rabbi Cohen hear his wife, Sarah, as she silently entered the room moments later. Putting on her night robe, she gingerly knelt at his side. Taking his hand in hers, she pressed firmly, then began a silent prayer of faith and *hope* that would sustain her through the night. For now, with the realization of her husband's condition, it was enough—

Dear Father, she began silently, *in the name of Thy holy son, Jesus, I ask a blessing on my Eli this night. And from a mother's broken, lonely heart, I also ask Thee to bless our Joseph. May he also . . . rest this night. And may he do so with a peace that passeth all understanding. It is my fervent prayer—*

Concluding, Sarah Cohen arose and slipped into bed. The springs creaked slightly, Rabbi Cohen caught his breath, and then in unison the two aging sweethearts breathed as one into the cool dank stillness of the night.

There was nothing between them—nothing, that is, except an ancient weathered piece of wood. It was a staff—for now the staff of life—and somehow it would survive the night without mishap. After all, it had work yet to do, and would resume its duties with the dawn of the next day.

Brenton G. Yorgason (left) and Richard G. Myers

ABOUT THE AUTHORS

Brenton Yorgason has authored or co-authored over seventy books. He has been a marriage and family therapist, and is founder and chairman of The Lincoln Institute. In this capacity, he speaks to organizations on *Mind Mastering: Managing Change from the Inside Out.* He and his wife, Margaret, are parents of nine children and three grand children, and reside in Provo, Utah.

Richard Myers was born and reared in Santa Monica, California. He lived in Italy for two years, and has studied in the field of psychology. A father of six, Richard and his wife, Susan, reside with their family in Spokane, Washington.

Previous to this work, Brenton and Richard co-authored the bestsellers, *Simeon's Touch, The Garrity Test, The Carpenter's Son (Book One),* and *The Last Stagecoach Robbery.*

For further information about The Lincoln Institute, as well as books authored or co-authored by Brenton and Richard, contact:

www.thelincolninstitute.com